Alison Moore was born in Manchester in 1971. Her stories have been published in various magazines and anthologies including *Best British Short Stories 2011*. She has been shortlisted for the Bridport Prize and the Manchester Fiction Prize, and for the Scott Prize for her first collection. She won first prize in the novella category of *The New Writer* Prose and Poetry Prizes. She lives near Nottingham with her husband Dan and son Arthur.

THE
LIGHTHOUSE

ALISON
MOORE

SALT

CROMER

PUBLISHED BY SALT PUBLISHING
12 Norwich Road, Cromer, Norfolk NR27 0AX United Kingdom

First published by Salt Publishing, 2012
Reprinted 2012

Printed in Great Britain by Clays Ltd, St Ives plc

Typeset in Paperback 9.5/14.5

ISBN 978 1 97773 17 4 paperback

3 5 7 9 8 6 4

for Mum and Dad

THE LIGHTHOUSE

she became a tall lighthouse sending out kindly beams which some took for welcome instead of warnings against the rocks

– Muriel Spark, 'The Curtain Blown by the Breeze'

CHAPTER ONE

VIOLETS

Futh stands on the ferry deck, holding on to the cold railings with his soft hands. The wind pummels his body through his new anorak, deranges his thinning hair and brings tears to his eyes. It is summer and he was not expecting this. He has not been on a ferry since he was twelve, when he went abroad for the first time with his father. It was summer then too and the weather was just as rough so perhaps this should not be taking him by surprise.

His father took him to the ferry's cinema. Futh does not remember what they saw. When they sat down, the lights were still up and there was no one else in there. He remembers having a bucket of warm popcorn on his lap. His father, smelling of the lager he had drunk beforehand at the bar, turned to Futh to say, 'Your mother sold popcorn.'

She had been gone for almost a year by then, by the time Futh and his father took this holiday together. Mostly, she was not mentioned, and Futh longed for his father or anybody to say, 'Your mother . . .' so that his heart would lift. But then, when she was spoken about, she would invariably be spoiled in some way and he would wish that nothing had been said after all.

'In those days,' his father said, 'the usherettes wore high heels as part of the uniform.'

Futh, shifting in his seat and burying his hand in his popcorn, hoped that the film or at least the trailers, even adverts, would start soon. Some people came in and sat down nearby, but his father went on just the same.

'I was there on a date. The girl I was with didn't want anything but I did. I went down the aisle to the front where your mother stood with her tray all lit up by the bulb inside. She sold me a bag of popcorn and agreed to meet me the following night.'

The lights went down and Futh, tensed in the dark auditorium, hoped that that would be it, that the story would end there.

His father leaned closer and lowered his voice. 'I drove her up to the viewpoint,' he said. 'She had this very pale skin which glowed in the moonlight and I half-expected her to feel cold. She was warm though – it was my hands that were chilly.'

The screen lit up and Futh tried to focus on that, on the fanfare and the flicker of light on expectant faces, and his father said, 'She complained about my cold hands but she didn't stop me. She wasn't uptight like some of the girls I'd taken up there.'

Futh felt the warm pressure of his father's thigh against his own, felt the tickle of his father's arm hairs on his own bare forearm, the heat of his father's beery breath in his ear hole, his father's hand reaching into his lap, taking popcorn. Finally, his father sat quietly back in his seat to watch the start of the film and after a few minutes Futh could tell by the sound of his breathing that his father had fallen asleep.

When his father woke up halfway through the film, he wanted to know what he had missed, but Futh, whose mind had been wandering, could not really tell him.

Ferries make Futh feel a bit sick. He becomes nauseous just thinking about walking through the bars and restaurants with their clashing textiles, sitting down at a dishcloth-damp table, the smell of other people's warm food lingering beneath the tang of cleaning fluids, his stomach roiling. He prefers to be outside in the fresh air.

It is nippy though. He does not have enough layers on. He has not put a jumper in the overnight bag which is stowed between his feet. He has not packed a jumper at all. Waves smack the hull of the boat, splashes and salt smell flying up. He can feel the rumble of the engine, the vibrations underfoot. He looks up at the night sky, up towards the waxing moon, inhaling deeply through his nose as if he can catch its scent in the wind, as if he can feel its pull.

Now the ramp is being raised like a drawbridge. He is reminded of the closing leaves of a Venus flytrap, but this is slower and noisier.

The mooring ropes are dropped into the water and Futh, like a disconcerted train passenger unable to tell whether it is his or a neighbouring train which is pulling out of the station, sees the untethered land drawing away from him. The engine chugs and the water churns white between the dock and the outward bound ferry.

There is someone else up on the outer deck, on the far side of a life ring, a man wearing a raincoat and a hat. As Futh glances at him, the man's hat blows off and lands in the sea, in their wake. The man turns and, noticing Futh, laughs and shouts something across the deck, against the wind. His words are lost but Futh gives an affable laugh in response. The man moves along the railings, holding on as if he might blow away as well. Arriving at Futh's side, the man says, 'Even so, I prefer to be outside.'

'Yes,' says Futh, catching the smell of the man's supper coming from his mouth, 'me too.'

'I get a little . . .' says the man, pressing the palm of his hand soothingly against his large stomach.

'Yes,' says Futh, 'me too.'

'I'm worse on aeroplanes.'

Futh and his companion stand and watch Harwich receding, the black sea rising and falling in the moonlight.

'Are you on holiday?' asks the man.

'Yes,' says Futh, 'I'm going walking in Germany.'

When Futh tells the man that he will be walking at least fifteen miles a day for a week, doing almost a hundred miles in total, the man says, 'You must be very fit.'

'I should be,' says Futh, 'by the end of the week. I don't walk much these days.'

The man reaches into the inside pocket of his coat, takes out a programme and hands it to Futh. 'I'm on my way to a conference,' he says, 'in Utrecht.'

Futh glances at the programme before passing it back – carefully in the bluster – saying, 'I don't really believe in that sort of thing.'

'No,' says the man, putting it away again, 'well, I'm undecided.' He pauses before adding, 'I'm also visiting my mother who lives in Utrecht. I'm dropping in on her first. I don't get over very often. She'll have been cooking all week, just for the two of us. You know how mothers are.'

Futh, watching the sea fill the growing gap between them and England, says, 'Yes, of course.'

'You're just going for a week?' says the man.

'Yes,' says Futh. 'I go home on the Saturday.'

'Same here,' says the man. 'I'll have had enough by then, enough of her fussing around me and feeding me. I put on a couple of kilos every time I'm there.'

Futh puts his hand in his coat pocket, wrapping his fingers around his keycard. 'I think I'm going to go to my room now,' he says.

'Well,' says the man, pulling back his coat cuff to check the time, 'it's almost midnight.' Futh admires the man's smart watch and the man says, 'It was a gift from my mother. I've told her she spends too much money on me.'

Futh looks at his own watch, a cheap one, a knock-off, which appears to be fast. He winds it back to just before midnight, back to the previous day. He says goodnight and turns away.

He is halfway across the deck when there is a tannoy announcement, a warning of winds of force six or seven, a caution not to risk going outside. He climbs down the steps, holding on to the handrail, and steadies himself against the walls until he reaches the door, which looks like an airlock. He goes through it into the lounge.

The floor is gently heaving. He feels it tilting and

dropping away beneath him. He walks unsteadily across the room towards the stairs and goes down, looking for his level, following the signs pointing him down the corridors to his cabin.

He lets himself in with his keycard and closes the door behind him, putting his overnight bag down on a seat just inside. He takes off his coat and hangs it on a hook on the back of the door just above the fire action notice. It is a small cabin with not much more than the seat and a desk, a cupboard, bunk beds on the far side, and a shower room. There is no window, no porthole. He looks inside the cupboard, half-expecting a trouser press or a little fridge or a safe, finding empty hangers. He does not need a trouser press but he would quite like a drink, a continental beer. He opens the door to the shower room and finds a plastic-wrapped cup by the sink. He fills the cup from the tap and takes his drink over to the bunk beds. Switching on the wall-mounted bedside lamp and turning off the overhead light, he sits down on the bottom bunk to take off his shoes.

Peeling off his socks, he massages his feet, which are sore from walking around the ferry and standing so long, braced, on the outer deck. He once knew a girl who did reflexology, who could press on the sole of his foot with her thumbs knowing that here was his heart and here was his pelvis and here was his spleen and so on.

Standing again, he takes a small, silver lighthouse out of his trouser pocket and places it in a side pocket of his overnight bag where it will not roll around and get lost. He locates his travel clock, takes off his watch, and undresses. He has new pyjamas and buries his nose in the fabric, in the 'new clothes' smell of formaldehyde, before putting them on. Taking out his wash bag, he goes into the shower room.

He watches himself brushing his teeth in the mirror over the sink. He looks tired and pale. He has been drinking too much and not eating enough and sleeping badly. He cups his hands beneath the cold running water, rinses out his mouth and washes his face. When he straightens up again, reaching for a towel, water drips down the front of his pyjamas.

He imagines coming home, his reflection in the mirror on the return journey, his refreshed and tanned self after a week of walking and fresh air and sunshine, a week of good sausage and deep sleep.

Back in the bedroom, he climbs the little ladder up to the top bunk, gets in between the sheets and switches off the lamp. He lies on his back with the ceiling inches from his face and tries to think about something other than the rolling motion of the ferry. The mattress seems to swell and shift beneath him like a living creature. There is a vent in the ceiling, from which cold, stale air leaks. He turns onto his side, trying not to think about Angela, who is perhaps even now going through his things and putting them in boxes, sorting out what to keep and what to throw away. The ferry ploughs on across the North Sea, and home gets further and further away. The cold air from the vent seeps down the neck of his pyjama top and he turns over again. His heart feels like the raw meat it is. It feels like something peeled and bleeding. It feels the way it felt when his mother left.

'I'm going home,' she said, meaning New York, meaning three thousand miles away. It was only after she had gone that Futh realised she had not left an address. He looked on the pin board in the kitchen but all he found was the start of a shopping list, her handwriting an almost flat line, a dash of Biro, indecipherable.

He looked in the library for pictures of New York, finding skyscrapers with suns rising and setting in their mirrored windows and all lit up at night, the light reflected in the river.

On his father's side, there was German, although his father had never been to Germany until they went there together when Futh was twelve. Futh's granddad had left home young, could not get away quickly enough. He settled in England and did not see his parents or his brother again.

'He never went home for a visit?' asked Futh.

'No,' said his father. 'He thought about it a lot, but he never made it home.'

Futh did not like to think that someone would just leave, and so abruptly, and never see their family again.

Abandoning the top bunk, Futh feels his way down the ladder to the bed underneath, and the cold air follows him.

He woke in the night and his mother was there, her round face above him, lit by the moon through a gap in the curtains. When she left his room he was alone in the dark with her scent – the smell of violets – and the sound of her footsteps going down the stairs.

By breakfast time, she was gone, and his father was already drunk. Before she left, his father never hit him.

Afterwards, when he did, it was without warning, or nothing Futh noticed in time. It was like when birds flew into windows with a sudden sickening thud, and then having to look at the bird lying terribly still on the ground outside, perhaps only dazed but probably hurt or broken in some way.

Futh tried not to get under his father's feet. Sometimes he stayed outside, sitting on top of his climbing frame until it was so dark he could not see the ground underneath, and the lawn could have been an ink-black lake or just a big nothing into which, jumping down, he would drop. He was safe out there – but in the darkness he could always see the bright square of the kitchen window.

Watching his father wandering around the kitchen, picking things out of the fridge and sniffing them, looking in the cupboards and opening a tin, lighting a hob, Futh would know when it was time to go in for supper. If he waited too long, the supper would go cold and everything would be spoilt. Or, watching his father sitting alone at a bare table, he would know to wait until his father went out before going in and putting himself to bed.

In the other direction, over the fence at the bottom of the garden, was Gloria's house. Futh had been friends with Gloria's son Kenny since the first year of junior school, even though they had little in common. Futh was not really a people person, while Kenny always had girls or a gang of boys around him. Kenny played football and army while Futh was in the school library waiting for breaktime to end. Kenny went orienteering with his father, and could build a bike from scratch. When Futh took his own bike apart and could not put it back together again his father refused to help. In the end, Futh put all the bits – the gears and the chain and the pedals and so on – into a box in the shed and kept them there thinking that one day he would know how to do it.

Kenny and Futh used to stand at their bedroom windows at lights out, facing one another across their back gardens, each with a torch, flashing messages through the darkness. It was like Morse code except that it didn't mean anything. Kenny would flash-flash-flash and Futh would flash-flash-flash back; Kenny would flash-pause-flash and Futh would send it back. Eventually, the game would stop. It was, for Futh, like looking at a lighthouse on the horizon at night. There was this flashing of light and then nothing, and you waited for the next flash, looking at where the light had been and where it would be again but you were looking at darkness.

When eventually no flash of light interrupted the darkness, it meant that Kenny was in bed, and then Futh got into bed too. In later years he would take the torch under the covers with him and read the sometime banned literature from his mother's bookshelves.

Halfway through junior school, Kenny left – his father moved out and Kenny went with him. It happened suddenly, with nobody telling Futh that Kenny was going or that he had gone, and Futh spent some nights at his bedroom window waiting to see Kenny's torch, wielding his own, flash-flash-flash, like a mating signal, receiving no reply.

Futh did not see Kenny again until Christmas. They met

at the butcher's. Gloria, coming into the shop and standing in line behind Futh and his mother, said hello. Kenny had already gone to wait outside and Futh joined him. Futh asked Kenny why he had left, and Kenny looked at him as if he were stupid and said, 'I went with my dad.'

'But why did your dad leave?' asked Futh.

'Well, he couldn't stay,' said Kenny, 'knowing about the affair, could he?'

When primary school ended and Futh's mother left and Futh began to spend his free time sitting on his climbing frame in the dark, he found himself thinking about Kenny, whom he had not seen in the two years since their meeting at the butcher's. He looked at Kenny's empty bedroom window, underneath which Gloria ate her supper alone in the kitchen.

She never seemed to have friends over, female friends like his mother had, who used to gather in the living room or on the patio in good weather, and sometimes his mother played a favourite song, her favourite singer, and started dancing, while he played by himself nearby, told to stay out of the way, getting as close as he dared, mesmerised by the noise and the perfume and the minidressed legs of his mother's friends. Gloria had not been one of them.

He got to know Gloria's habits. When she came into the kitchen to prepare her evening meal, she would turn on the radio. She would open the back door to call in the cat and feed it titbits from her plate while she was eating. When she finished, she would clear up and then, leaving the radio on, she would go upstairs to take a shower or a bath, and he would see her, the vague pinkness of her, fragmented by the bathroom window's bobbled glass. She would come back down in her nightie, sit at the kitchen table and have a drink or two. She would feed the cat again, maybe take out the rubbish, or, in that summer of drought, soak her garden with the hosepipe in the dark. Alone in a street full of parched and pale lawns, while neighbours' plants wilted and died, Gloria's garden was lush.

The back door opened and Gloria appeared on her doorstep with a rubbish bag, but instead of going to the bins she walked onto the lawn, coming his way in her nightie, bringing the rubbish bag with her.

Leaning against the fence, she said, 'All on your lonesome?'

Not knowing what to say, Futh said nothing.

'Me too,' she said, twirling the rubbish bag in her hand. 'I could do with some company.'

'I've got to go in soon,' said Futh.

Gloria looked over Futh's shoulder at the house, at the lit kitchen window. 'What you and your daddy need now,' she said, 'is a nice holiday. That's what I did when my husband left me. I went off on holiday. After a fortnight of sunshine and cocktails, I wasn't even thinking about him.'

Futh, hearing his father calling him, turned around and was beckoned inside. When Futh turned back, Gloria was already walking away with her rubbish bag.

'What did she want?' asked his father, as Futh stepped into the kitchen.

'She just came over to talk to me,' said Futh.

'What did she say?'

'She said she was lonely.'

'I don't want you talking to her,' said his father.

There were bowls of oxtail soup on the table. They sat down and ate, and Futh, through the curtainless window and across the dark back gardens, saw Gloria's kitchen light and all her downstairs lights go off. A minute later, he saw her bathroom light go on again.

There was a curtain rail there, above the kitchen window. When they moved into this house, when Futh was seven, his mother had measured up for curtains, but she never got round to making them before she left. She had planned to paint the house from top to bottom, but had only done the landing when she stopped and did no more. Most of the pictures she brought from the old house were never hung, and the flowerbeds were planted but then grew wild.

His father, polishing off his oxtail soup, standing and reaching for his slip-on shoes, said, 'I'm going out. Finish up, it's your bedtime.' When he opened the kitchen door, the cold night air came in and stayed when he was gone.

Gloria's bathroom light went off and Futh saw Gloria coming into her bedroom. He shovelled his soup, chasing the last bits of meat around the bottom of the bowl. He saw her in front of her dressing table mirror, checking the look of herself in her nightie, touching her hair. She went back out onto the landing. A moment later, the light in the downstairs hallway went on, and when it went off again Futh stood quickly, put his empty soup bowl in the sink and went to bed.

He wakes in darkness. He can't see a thing and doesn't know where he is.

'Where am I?' he asks, before grasping that he is alone. He thinks he must be in the spare room, but everything feels wrong. Then he thinks he might be in his second-hand bed at the new flat but that does not seem right either. Finally he realises that he is on the ferry. He is on holiday, he thinks, that's all, he is going on holiday, and he goes back to sleep.

He and his father had a daytime crossing to Europe. As well as taking him to the cinema and letting him have popcorn, his father bought him sweets in a mug from the duty-free shop and too many packets of peanuts at the bar and Futh felt sick in the car all the way from the ferry to their hotel in Germany.

Their hotel room had two single beds and a small bathroom. At bedtime, when Futh wanted a night light, his father put the bathroom light on and left the door ajar, and then said, 'Go to sleep now.' But Futh lay awake, turned towards that crack of light, watching in the big mirror behind the sink as his father changed his shirt and combed his hair and brushed his teeth and then – Futh quickly closing his eyes and trying to breathe like someone sleeping – he left, the door clicking shut behind him.

In the morning, his father would be there, in the other single bed, dozing with his mouth open, the odour of alcohol seeping out. When Futh got out of bed to go to the bathroom, his father would stir, asking, with eyes narrowed against the daylight, what time it was. Futh would tell him, and his father would be surprised by how late it was. He would say to Futh, 'You slept well.' And Futh would say nothing about when, disturbed in the early hours, he saw the bedroom door opening, the light coming in from the corridor, his father returning with a woman, a different woman every night. When the door shut behind them, his father and these women felt their way through the bedroom still dimly lit by the light from the bathroom into which his father took them, the bathroom light briefly flooding the bedroom before the door was again closed leaving only the narrow gap through which Futh watched them in the mirror. And Futh, who had not slept well, stood in the bathroom in the morning, not wanting to touch the sink area, not wanting to look in the mirror.

He said nothing to his father about having woken up to find himself wetting the bed. He pulled his blanket over the wet sheets and got ready to go out, knowing that it would all be made clean in his absence.

Futh opens his eyes in the dark and hears a woman speaking to him loudly in a language he does not understand. He squints in the direction of his travel clock, trying to make sense of the position of the luminous hands. He can't see the underside of the bunk right above him, and he reaches out and touches it to reassure himself that he is where he thinks he is. Then, feeling for the switch on the wall, he turns on the light.

It is morning and the ferry is arriving into the Hook of Holland. Futh gets up.

In the shower, in an apple-scented lather, he thinks about Angela. He wonders what she did with her Friday night and what she is planning to do with her Saturday.

They have spent most of their Friday evenings on the sofa watching television. Now, early on a Saturday morning, he imagines her barely home from a night out, or in bed asleep, or not asleep, with another man. It is more than fifteen years since he was with anyone else.

Turning off the shower and stepping out of the cubicle onto the non-slip floor, he finds himself still thinking about his father and the women in the hotel bathroom. He leans against the sink area, wipes his hand over the steamed-up mirror and looks again at his reflection. He does not see his father in himself.

Back in the bedroom, he dresses, returning the silver lighthouse to his trouser pocket. He goes around collecting up the complimentary items – a Biro, sachets of coffee and sugar and individual portions of UHT milk, the remaining toiletry miniatures, a shower cap, the plastic cup – and packs them in his overnight bag. He can make use of all these things in his new flat.

He leaves his cabin, taking his bag and his anorak with him, not wanting to have to come back. He goes to look for some breakfast, but when he is standing at the edge of the restaurant, eyeing the queue and smelling the warm egg, the warm meat, he changes his mind. Instead, putting on his anorak and shouldering his bag, he heads for the outer deck.

It has been raining and is still raining behind them, mizzling into the sea. The metal steps are slippery and he has to go carefully. The sky overhead is a pale grey but it is clearing up over Holland as they draw near. He stands with his hands on the wet railings, watching the ferry's arrival into the Dutch terminal, and on the other side of the deck, the man in the raincoat who lost his hat does the same.

Futh moves his watch on an hour. Now he will go down to the car deck. When he is waved forward, he will drive out onto the continent, behind the wheel in another country for the first time.

'Not long now.'

Futh turns and finds the man standing beside him.

'Where in Germany are you going?' asks the man.

'Hellhaus,' says Futh. 'Near Koblenz. It's quite a long drive.'

'Oh, it won't take you long,' says the man. 'A few hours.'

'If I don't go wrong,' says Futh, picturing the pristine European road atlas on his passenger seat. Angela has always done the long-distance driving and is also the better navigator.

The ferry is docking. 'We should head down to the car deck,' says Futh.

'I'm on foot,' says the man.

'Where did you say you're going?'

'Utrecht. It's not far from here. You'll go right past it on your way to Koblenz. You should stop there for coffee if you have time.'

Futh looks at the man's damp coat, smells the rain trapped in its weave. He looks at the residue of rain on the man's eyelashes, on his eyebrows, on his bare head. He imagines this man in his passenger seat, reading the map and knowing the roads. He says, 'Would you like a lift to Utrecht?'

The man beams. 'Well,' he says, 'if you're going there

anyway, that would be very kind. You can have coffee at my mother's house.'

'I'd like that,' says Futh, 'very much.'

The man holds out his hand and says, 'Carl.'

Carl's hand is big and tanned and, Futh finds as he takes it, warm. Futh's own hand – slim and pale and cold – seems lost inside it. 'Futh,' he says in reply. Carl leans closer, turning one ear towards him as if he has not quite caught it, and Futh has to say again, 'Futh.'

The two men turn away from the railings to head inside together. The boat's wet surfaces gleam in the early morning sunlight, and Futh wonders how long the ferry will stay in the brightening port before turning around and going out again, back out into the cold, grey sea.

CHAPTER TWO

BREASTS

Ester gets herself comfortable on her high stool at the bar and removes her rubber gloves. She adds a little tonic to the shot of gin in front of her and drinks it down. She likes to have her first drink of the day when she finishes the downstairs rooms.

It is just after eleven. It is always quiet at this time, just before lunch. There is only herself and the new girl and one customer, a man at the other end of the bar. She is aware of him staring at her but she does not turn and look at him, not yet.

When she puts down her glass, she spots a smear on the rim, a red lipstick stain which is not hers. She calls the new girl over, holding out the glass for her to see, but the girl just takes it, thinking only that she is being given Ester's dirty glass.

Ester sits with one foot resting on the crossbar of her stool and the other foot touching the floor, a position which makes her look as if she is on the point of going somewhere, but she is not. She can see herself reflected in the mirrors behind the bottles on the shelves. She spent a long time that morning at her dressing table trying to get her face right, but she can see, looking at herself now in the space between two bottles of mediocre red wine, that the make-up around her right eye and on her cheekbone is too heavy.

Her vest top shows off the bruises on her upper arms, rows of dark ovals like smudgy police station fingerprints, as well as her slackening bosom and the tattoo above her left breast – a rose, fully open, the petals loose and beginning to drop. Her top's thin straps sink into her flesh, which is pale and doughy like uncooked pastry.

Now she looks at him, at the lone customer, a middle-aged man standing a few metres away. His broad shoulders are rounded, hunched over the bar. With his flat backside and short, thin legs, he makes the shape of a question mark. He is drinking a cup of coffee and peeling a hard-boiled egg, still watching her.

Ester, speaking German, says, 'You're not a guest here.'

'No,' he says. 'I came in for breakfast.' Making small talk, he moves up the bar towards her with his naked egg, the white giving between his broad thumb and his short fingers. He stands so close that his foot is touching hers, but she doesn't move hers away. He bites into his egg and she hears it being wetly masticated inside his mouth.

She fingers her hair, which is yellowy like the rubber gloves, like the crumbly egg yolk. She says, 'I have to get back to work. I'm just taking a break.'

'I have places to be as well,' he says, and Ester sees the eggy, claggy inside of his opening and closing mouth. 'I'm just passing through.'

She notices the butterfly tattoo on the back of his other hand, the hand which is not holding the egg, the thumb of which is hooked into his belt at the buckle. She gets down from her stool and walks to the internal door which leads to the guest rooms, glancing back at him before going through.

The man puts the last of the egg in his mouth and follows her, leaving the broken eggshell behind him on the bar.

He lies on his back in a bed which was vacated that morning by an American couple, whose dark hairs Ester can still see on the pillowcases. He is looking brazenly, unblinkingly, at her breasts and nothing else.

In her flat-chested youth, Ester collected pictures of other young women's breasts in a scrapbook – breasts in bras from the underwear pages of her mother's catalogues, breasts in bikinis from travel brochures, bare breasts from the plastic surgery adverts at the back of her mother's magazines and from the magazines her father kept under his side of the mattress. As a teenager, she spent a great deal of time poring over these pictures of coveted breasts. Now nearing forty, she has almost forgotten this phase, but this man's gaze reminds her of herself in her bedroom with her scrapbook on her lap. She gets onto the bed, and he does not take his eyes off her breasts, and she does not really look at him at all, looks near him, past him. When he has finished, he closes his eyes and falls asleep.

He was quick, but that's just as well. Ester still has two rooms to do before lunchtime. There are toilets and sinks and baths to be cleaned, floors to be mopped, carpets to be vacuumed, beds to be made, including the one they are lying in.

In the past, she always used beds she had already changed, but since receiving complaints about the sheets, she makes sure to use rooms she has not yet cleaned. Or she uses rooms whose occupants are out for the day, brushing off and straightening up the bedding afterwards, and sometimes, while she is there, browsing the contents of drawers and suitcases, picking up perfumes and lipsticks, testing them on herself. If guests ever notice their possessions, these small items, going missing, they rarely say anything.

Ester looks at the man lying asleep at her side. He is turned towards her, the ends of his fingers resting on her arm, just touching her, his butterfly still reaching for her spoiling rose. He has a crumb of egg yolk in the stubble at the corner of his mouth. She moves away, and his fingertips slip from her skin.

Sitting on the edge of the mattress, she leans down and gathers her clothes from the floor. She puts them on, picking off hairs.

His jeans lie tangled at the end of the bed and she reaches for them, going through his pockets and finding a packet of cigarettes and a red Bic lighter. She takes a cigarette to the open window to light it, leaning her bare elbows on the sill and watching the people going by down below. When she exhales, her smoke puffs out over their heads like bad weather.

Dropping the burning cigarette end out of the window, not waiting to see it land, to see the sparks as it hits the pavement, she turns away. She pauses in front of a full-length mirror to tidy her hair and her face, the smeared pink of her lipstick. Then, slipping her feet into her flats, she leaves the room.

She is a few steps away from the still-closing door when she sees Bernard arrive at the top of the stairs at the other end of the corridor. He looks her way, sees her, and holds up the rubber gloves which she left on the bar beside her tonic bottle. She walks steadily towards him, takes the gloves and thanks him, and then fetches the cleaning cart she has already sent up in the lift. Wheeling it into the next bedroom, room six, she is aware of Bernard watching her before turning and going back down the stairs to the bar.

Ester goes first into the small en suite bathroom and picks up the used towels which have been left damp on the floor. She sprays disinfectant onto a cloth and wipes down the toilet, pours bleach into the bowl. She cleans the bath, pulling a clump of hair from the plughole. Rinsing her cloth and squirting more disinfectant, she polishes the sink and the tooth glass. She mops the lino, straightens the shower curtain, puts out clean towels and complimentary soap.

In the bedroom, she strips the sheet from the bed, shakes it out and inspects it and then smooths it over the mattress again. She turns over the pillows, plumping them up. She wipes down the laminate furniture, hoovers the carpet and sprays the room with air freshener. As she unplugs the vacuum cleaner, she hears footsteps in the corridor, heavy shoes coming from the far end, passing the door of the room she is in and going down the stairs.

She centres the vase of plastic flowers on the dressing

table and puts a sachet of instant coffee, an individual portion of UHT milk and a packet of two plain biscuits by the kettle and a mint on one of the pillows.

She pushes her cleaning trolley out into the corridor and down to the far end, fetching clean bedding from her linen cupboard. She opens the door to room ten and finds the messy bed vacated, the bathroom empty.

Downstairs, the question mark steps through the door leading from the guest rooms into the bar. Thinking about having another drink but deciding against it, he crosses the room and exits into the street, into the midday heat, walking away in the shade. Bernard, standing behind the bar, watches him go.

Ester is expecting a Mr Futh to arrive in time for lunch, and a honeymoon couple around four. The rooms are ready and she has asked the kitchen to prepare a plate of cold meats for Mr Futh. Fetching herself a measure of gin and a fresh bottle of tonic from behind the bar, she sits down on her stool and waits for her guests to arrive.

CHAPTER THREE

BEEF AND ONION

'Do you ever get a bad feeling about something?' says Carl. 'A bad feeling about something that's going to happen?'

'Sure,' says Futh. 'I used to get panic attacks on aeroplanes.'

'I'm not keen on flying,' says Carl. 'I was once on a plane and had a really uneasy feeling and had to get off again. I don't like being underground either. I avoid the tube and the Channel Tunnel.'

'One time,' says Futh, 'I was flying to New York and while the plane was taking off I couldn't stop imagining there being a fire or a terrorist on board and not being able to escape.'

'What happened?'

'Oh, nothing. It was fine, you know. I used a relaxation technique.'

Carl frowns and says, 'But I mean, do you ever sense that something's going to happen and then it does?'

'Oh yes,' says Futh. 'Last Christmas, I visited my dad and

his girlfriend, and I just knew he was going to be in a bad mood, and he was.'

Futh drives forward, off the ferry, following the car in front. They are waved on by officials in orange waterproofs. They sail through customs, passing others whose cars are being emptied, and through passport control. Then they are off, away.

Futh says, 'And I know I'll spend next Christmas with them too, and it will be just as bad.'

Carl nods, but he is still frowning. 'Why don't you spend the week in Utrecht with me and my mother?'

'A whole week?' asks Futh. 'At Christmas?'

'I mean this week,' says Carl. 'I'm attending this conference midweek but my mother would look after you.'

'Oh,' says Futh, and he is thoughtful for a moment before saying, 'That's very kind of you, but I have all my accommodation booked.'

'My mother would love to have you stay and I'll only be gone for a few days, I'll be back on Friday evening. We could travel together on the Saturday. Are you on the late ferry?'

Futh says that he is and again he muses for a while before saying that he would like to but cannot.

Carl is quiet. He seems troubled and Futh wonders whether Carl is offended.

'I'll see you on the ferry though?' says Futh.

Carl gives the slightest nod.

Futh hopes that his driving is not bothering Carl. In explanation, as they get onto the motorway, Futh mentions to Carl that he has not been driving very long and has not done much motorway driving. 'And I've never driven abroad,' he says. He accelerates, moving out to overtake the thundering lorries, his small car trembling in the middle lane.

Prior to taking a driving test in his forties, Futh had relied mainly on public transport and hitchhiking. When Futh left home, his father sold the family house and moved in with his sister, Futh's Aunt Frieda. Futh, visiting, would hitch-hike there and back and Frieda, who did not approve of hitchhiking, warned him to watch out for strange men.

'And strange women,' added his father.

'Just be careful,' said Frieda.

Futh thought that she worried about him unduly. When he was little, when he climbed on rocks, when he was reck-less, trying to be like the other boys, she would say, 'You'll fall. You'll hurt yourself.' And then he would indeed fall and hurt himself and she would tell him, 'You're an accident waiting to happen.'

When she took him to the swimming pool, she made him wear armbands even though he told her he could swim. Sometimes he went to the river with Kenny, and later he went on his own. Frieda warned him against swim-ming in the river, because of the current and the weeds and the rocks, and there were parasites and diseases and God knows what in that river, she said, and every now and again someone drowned. When he last saw Frieda, some weeks before coming to Germany, she asked him not to go, not to drive all that way, not to walk all that way, not to go on his own. She telephoned the day he left to warn him to look after his feet, to keep his passport safe, to be careful. 'Stay away,' she said, 'from that river.'

'This is it,' says Carl, peering through the windscreen, pointing out the turn they need to take, their route off the motorway and into Utrecht.

Futh follows Carl's directions which take them to the far side of the city. They park by the kerb in front of an old three-storey house which has been divided into flats. Futh, out of the car, standing on the pavement, still feels the lurch of the ferry.

The front door has an intercom with three buttons, one of which Carl presses. There is a crackle and then a woman's voice speaking what Futh assumes to be Dutch.

'Mummy,' says Carl, speaking in English for Futh's benefit, 'it's Carl, and I have a guest.' When the door makes a clicking sound, Carl pushes it open and Futh follows him inside.

They climb the stairs up to the third-floor flat, to a door which has been opened and left ajar for them. They enter and Carl closes the door behind them. Hanging up his coat and turning to take Futh's, Carl calls, 'Mummy?' They walk through to the living room, Futh taking in the high ceilings, bare floorboards, wooden slatted blinds, sparse furniture, uncluttered surfaces, glass and leather and the smell of polish. Again Carl shouts, 'Mummy!' and the acoustics in the harshly furnished room are like those in an empty house or in a bathroom.

In the far corner, a swinging door opens and a woman comes into the room. The smells of coffee and baking follow her. She greets Carl with little air kisses while Futh stands waiting to be introduced. When Carl turns to him and says, 'Mummy, this is our guest, my friend,' Futh steps forward and kisses Carl's mother on one cheek and then the other, smelling soap and flowers beneath the coffee and the baking.

'I'm so pleased to meet you,' he says.

'You are very welcome,' says Carl's mother, turning away. 'Come and sit down.'

The three of them walk over to an uncomfortable-looking sofa and Futh sits down in the middle. On a low table in front of the sofa stands a tray, from which Carl's mother lifts a coffee pot. She fills three cups and passes the first one to Futh who takes it with a smile. She asks him about his journey and his holiday, and while he talks she listens and offers milk and sugar. Passing a plate of little pastries, she enquires about his wife, his children.

'My wife and I have just separated,' says Futh.

Expressing sympathy, she puts the plate of pastries down in front of him.

'And we didn't have children.' He shifts his buttocks on the thinly upholstered sofa.

'Perhaps that's just as well,' says Carl's mother.

'I keep stick insects,' he says. 'I wanted a dog.' Angela had said no to a dog. She did not want to end up being the one who had to walk it every day. So he got stick insects. He is rather fond of them but he supposes that they have no sense of him, that they do not remember him from one day to the next.

Carl's mother says to Carl, 'You aren't drinking your coffee. Has it gone cold?'

Carl, who has been taciturn all morning, ever since the conversation in the car, looks down at the untouched cup of coffee in his hand. He puts it down on the little table. 'If you'll excuse me,' he says, 'there is something I have to do.' He crosses the living room again, going back out into the hallway, his mother following him with her eyes.

After a moment, she turns back to Futh. 'More coffee?' she says, turning away to pour it, asking what he does for a living.

'I work in the manufacture of synthetic smells,' says Futh.

'Oh yes?' She looks glazed.

He elaborates. 'We artificially replicate the chemical compounds which make apples smell like apples and so on, mimicking natural smells. Have you heard of scratch and sniff? In scratch and sniff technology, the chemicals are captured in microscopic spheres, like tiny bottles of perfume. When a scratch and sniff panel is used, a few of the bottles are broken, but there are millions of them – after twenty years all the bottles will not be broken, the fragrance will not be gone.'

'Oh, I'm sure that's very interesting,' she says. She glances at her watch. 'And what does your father do?'

'He was a chemistry teacher,' says Futh. 'He's retired now.' He finishes his coffee and Carl's mother smiles and reaches out to take the cup from his hands. 'Thank you,' he says, glancing at the coffee pot.

She begins to stand, with Futh's empty cup in her hands, saying, 'Well, I'm sure you want to go on your way.'

'I'm not in any hurry,' says Futh. She hesitates, and then settles back down again. Futh shifts towards her and continues, his breath heavy with coffee. 'Everything you smell contains a volatile chemical, which evaporates and activates the nasal sensory cells. When you can smell something it's because it's releasing molecules into the air, which you inhale.'

'I have so much to do,' she says, and Futh begins to explain the rota system he and Angela used for housework.

Carl's mother seems distracted. From time to time, she glances towards the door through which Carl left. Suddenly, she stands up, saying, 'I know what he's doing.' She strides across the room and into the hallway. Futh hears her give a single knock on a door before entering. She closes the door behind her and Futh can hear her speaking angrily to Carl, although he can't make out what is being said.

When she returns she says to Futh, who is reaching out to take another pastry, 'Perhaps you should be going after that.' Futh, trying to choose between the remaining pastries, is only vaguely aware of Carl reentering the room. Carl's mother, already moving away from Futh towards the kitchen, says, 'Shall I pack you a lunch to take with you?'

'That won't be necessary,' he says. 'I'm due to have lunch in Hellhaus.'

'You won't be there for lunch,' she says.

Futh, who has lost track of the time and who in any case does not really know how long this leg of his journey will take, looks at his watch and sees how late in the morning it is. 'Well,' he says, smiling gratefully at his host, 'if that's the case then that would be very kind of you.'

She goes into the kitchen and Carl follows her.

Futh, left behind, perched on the edge of the terrible sofa, looks towards the kitchen door. When it swings open, he sees Carl quietly admonishing his mother. It swings to and then swings open again and he sees Carl's mother turning, making her hushed reply. They speak not only in low voices but in Dutch, and Futh does not understand a word. The swinging slows and stops. Futh is reminded of the scenes he tried not to hear as a child, his parents whispering furiously on the other side of closed doors.

Carl is the first to come out of the kitchen. 'Please,' he says, 'you don't have to go. My mother did not mean to make you feel unwelcome.'

'Well,' says Futh, eyeing the cooling coffee pot, 'I probably should get going.'

Carl's mother comes into the room holding a grease-proof-paper parcel. 'For your journey,' she says to Futh, presenting him with the package. He takes it, expecting it to be warm in his hands but finding it cold.

Carl follows him out into the hallway. 'You should stay,' he says. 'I really want you to stay.' Futh, putting on his coat, smiles and offers his hand. Carl takes it, holding it a little too long.

Futh calls back into the living room, 'Many thanks for your hospitality.' He waits for a reply but none comes. He leaves the apartment and climbs back down the stairs to the front door which closes heavily behind him as he steps out into the street carrying the cool parcel in both hands.

At noon, Futh finally makes his way out of Utrecht and gets back onto the motorway, driving in the direction of Hell-haus, which is the name of both the town to which he is heading and the hotel in which he will be staying, where he will spend both this first night and his last night.

As he drives south with his window down, his bare forearm, resting on the frame, burns.

After a couple of hours, he stops at a rest area to eat the meat pie which Carl's mother gave him, savouring it, the perfect pastry melting in his mouth, the meat juice running down his chin and onto the front of his short-sleeved shirt.

He remembers a picnic in Cornwall, a family summer holiday just before his mother left: beef and onion in pastry with a forkhole pattern, lukewarm in a greasy paper bag; sitting on a cliff in blazing sunshine, looking at a lighthouse and listening to his father going on about the old beacon built by a notorious wrecker, a plunderer of stranded ships.

He returns to the motorway and drives until the end of the afternoon when he realises that he has missed his turning some way back. Unable – on the motorway, in between junctions – to turn around, he presses on, going in the wrong direction, accelerating.

Futh recalls sitting in the passenger seat of Angela's car with a UK road atlas in his hands, looking on the map for the place names he saw signposted at each motorway exit they sped past, and it dawning on him that he was taking them the wrong way round the M25. He grew anxious but kept quiet, wanting to be mistaken, to be going the right way after all despite the mounting evidence to the con-trary. Angela said, 'This doesn't feel right,' but still he said nothing, putting off the moment when he would have to admit his mistake, when they would have to come off the motorway and go all the way back, and meanwhile just making things worse.

By the time he arrives at Hellhaus, it is dreadfully late. It is dark as he parks his car and walks up the street with his suitcase on wheels, heading towards the centre of the small town.

He has wondered whether this Hellhaus has similar origins to a Hellhaus he knows of in Saxony – the ruin of a structure sited at the intersection of forest paths, used in its day to see and signal the whereabouts of escaping game. But when he turns a corner and sees the hotel, he understands why it has this name, which translates as 'bright house' or 'light house'. Whitewashed and moonlit, it is incandescent.

He feels again the tipping sensation he has experienced on and off since leaving the ferry. It feels like his soul is sliding out and then sliding back in again. His insides feel like the jelly in his father's hot pork pies oozing through cracks in the crust.

He trudges up the final incline, exhausted from driving and hungry again, the hotel a beacon before him.

CHAPTER FOUR

PERFUME

When the door opens, letting in the cool night air and some noise from the street, Ester turns towards it. A man walks in, a thin, pale man with thinning, mousy hair. He carries an anorak over one arm, and with the other he is pulling a suitcase on wheels. The door closes quietly behind him and the exterior sounds are shut out.

She stays sitting on her stool, tidying pieces of orange peel into the saucer of her coffee cup. The man comes to the bar, approaching the new girl, the little wheels of his suitcase clackety-clacking over the floorboards. 'Futh,' he says to the girl, 'I'm Futh.' The girl looks at him, asks him in German what he wants. 'Ich bin Futh,' he says.

When the girl continues to look blankly at him, he turns and looks around the room. Ester, who has been waiting for him all afternoon and all evening, lets him come to her. Clackety-clack, clackety-clack, goes his suitcase over the wooden floor, clackety-clack like a train, trundling to a stop. He stands in front of her, and she regards him, this man with gravy on his chin and on his shirt and even on the crotch of his trousers. 'I'm Futh,' he says again in English. 'Someone's expecting me.'

Ester climbs down off her seat and walks over to her desk. He follows her, chattering away. He says, 'Are you Ester?' She would prefer something more formal but lets it go.

She ticks his name off in her ledger and takes his key from a row of small hooks on the wall. 'Room six,' she says, putting the key into his hand.

He says, 'Thank you, Ester.'

She takes the handle of his suitcase, wheels it into the hallway and presses the button to bring down the lift.

While Mr Futh is travelling up to the first floor, Ester goes to the kitchen to fetch the plate of cold cuts which was prepared for him at lunchtime and has been kept under clingfilm in the fridge since then.

She takes Mr Futh's supper plate up in the lift and knocks on his door. When there is no answer, she lets herself in with her master key.

He is not in the bedroom. She can hear the shower running in the bathroom, can hear him singing in there. She would prefer not to have to talk to this man who keeps calling her Ester as if he knows her. She is still annoyed with him for being so late and not even apologising. She is obliged to feed the man – she wants to feed him, she always wants to feed men – but she would be pleased to get away without having to engage with him.

She puts the plate of cold meats down on the bedside table and peels off the cling film. It looks a little dry, but that is his own fault. She turns to look at the suitcase which is open on the bed.

There is nothing of interest in there, just clothes, and a few books at the bottom. Except, in amongst the clothes in which he arrived, in the pocket of his gravy-stained trousers, there is a silver lighthouse. About ten centimetres tall and three or four in diameter, it fits rather nicely inside her encircling hand. It has a four-sided tower and a lantern room with tiny storm panes and a domed top. In relief on one side it says 'DRALLE', the name of an old Hamburg perfumery. This ornate silver case ought to contain a cut-glass vial of a very expensive perfume, but Ester finds that it is empty, the scent missing.

When Ester was a child, her mother worked for a toiletrics company, travelling a lot and leaving Ester with an au pair. Ester's mother always came home with samples in her luggage. Having worn the same scent all her adult life, she gave her unwanted vials of perfume to Ester who collected them in a box on her dressing table and used them liberally, often sitting down to breakfast with a different scent on each pulse point.

Ester wanted to be a perfumier. She knew the names of many perfume houses – old and new, large and small – and their fragrances. She decided to create her own scent and went through her mother's kitchen cupboards, combining lemon juice, peach juice, vanilla essence, herbs and spices, imagining that she was making the ultimate scent, one sniff of which would make someone fall in love with her. Completing it with shredded petals from her mother's prized rose bush, Ester went to her parents' bedroom and took her mother's perfume from the dressing table. She poured it – her mother's Eau de Parfum, her signature scent – down the sink and refilled the empty bottle with her own first perfume, a sticky concoction which she called 'Ester', presenting it as a gift to her mother when she came home.

Ester was given no more sample scents after that. The next person to give her perfume was Bernard.

Ester hears the shower being turned off, the shower curtain being drawn back, the clatter of the hoops being pulled along the rail. She drops the lighthouse back onto the pile of clothes and begins to leave. Halfway across the room, she hesitates, turns around and takes a step back towards the bed with her eye on the lighthouse. But she can hear him moving towards the bathroom door, still singing. She turns away again.

When the bathroom door opens, she is out in the corridor, heading for the stairs, the door to room six closing slowly behind her.

At the opposite end of the corridor, just past room ten, there is a door marked 'PRIVATE', and it divides the guest rooms from those occupied by Ester and her husband.

Bernard, coming through this door, sees his wife hurriedly leaving room six and heading downstairs. Moments later, a man appears in the doorway of the same room, leaning out and looking towards the stairs. The man is partially hidden behind the door, but Bernard sees a bare shoulder, the knobbles of the man's spine, a white leg, a blue-veined foot on the hallway carpet. The man turns his head and sees Bernard and withdraws into his room looking embarrassed. The door clicks shut and a key is turned in the lock.

In the night, there will be a storm. It will be brief, if a little violent, and hardly anyone will even realise it has occurred, although they might hear it raging, thundering, in their dreams.

In the morning, by the time people are up and about, the sun will be out again, and the rain-soaked pavements will be dry, and there will be very little evidence of damage.

CHAPTER FIVE

SUN CREAM

In the small, low-ceilinged bathroom, Futh fills his tooth glass at the sink and takes big gulps before realising that he is drinking water from the hot tap. He has heard the stories about people finding dead pigeons in hot water tanks. He pours away what is left and refills his glass with cold water, which he still does not much like the taste of. He goes back to the bedroom. It is very early – he woke, thirsty, long before his alarm – but it is light and he could do with an early start anyway.

The night before, his supper miraculously appeared in his room while he was taking a shower. He ate in his pyjamas, standing at the window, looking out at the river.

He has got into the habit of always determining an escape route from a room in which he is staying, imagining emergency scenarios in which his exit is blocked by fire or a psychopath. This began, he thinks, when he was in his twenties and living in an attic flat. His Aunt Frieda, worrying about stair fires and burglars, gave him a rope ladder. It seems important that he should always know a way out.

Putting down his supper plate, he opened the window – looking, in the dark, for a roof to climb on to, a pipe to hold on to, a soft landing – and a moth flew in. Underneath the window, there was pavement, and it looked a long way down. He wondered if it was possible to jump from such a height without breaking anything.

Having finished his meal, he brushed and flossed his teeth and went straight to bed. Finding a mint on his pillow, he heard his Aunt Frieda in his head warning him about tooth decay, the dangers of sweets, but he ate it anyway, sucking it down to nothing.

He opened a book and tried to read but could not concentrate, kept reading the same lines over and over and reaching the bottom of the first page without having taken it in. He was distracted by the moth flying at his lamp. He got out of bed again and opened the curtains and the window to let it out, knowing that this disoriented moth was really after the moon, its navigational aid, although Futh could not see the moon from where he was standing. Getting back into bed, he turned over his pillow to get the cool side and noticed the stain of a stranger's mascara like a spider on his pillowcase. He resumed his reading and the moth flew away from the lamplight, the artificial light, towards the open window.

Still his thoughts drifted, towards home and Angela and where he had gone wrong. She had always been irritated by his awkwardness around people, around women in particular. He knew her mother found him strange. He was introspective, insufficiently aware, Angela often said, of other people and how they might see things.

The moth flew out of a fold in the curtains and back towards the lamplight, bumping and fluttering against the hot bulb. Futh shut his book and put it down on the bedside table. He got up to find the map he would need for the next day's walk and lay down again to study his route. But he could not stop thinking about all the ways in which he had annoyed his wife during their marriage.

He was a bad listener, apparently, bewilderingly incapable sometimes of following simple instructions. He was always late leaving the house, late arriving anywhere, even when he had to meet Angela. And he never apologised, even when he was clearly in the wrong. These were small things but he supposed they built up, amounted to something. He imagined things being different. He had a reverie in which he said and did the right thing and Angela did not leave him. But it was too late, it had already happened.

Having nodded off with the light on, and having slept deeply before waking early with the map creased under his cheek, Futh now stands once more at the window looking down at the quiet street below. There is not yet anybody about and nothing is open. It is, he realises, not only early, it is also a Sunday.

He turns away from the window and in the early morning light he notices the colour of the bedroom walls, which are painted a deep pink – the colour of rare meat, the colour of his sunburnt arm.

He dresses for the day's hiking, strapping his watch onto his unburnt wrist and putting the silver lighthouse in the pocket of his shorts. He goes downstairs, taking his supper plate with him. The landlady is sitting on her stool at the bar with her back to him, drinking a cup of coffee and eating an orange. He approaches her, putting his dirty plate down on the bar in front of her, thanking her in German. She turns, and he sees the new bruise on her face, despite the make-up she has applied. He thanks her again and she nods. He stands for a moment just smiling. He thinks to ask her about breakfast but before he has put the sentence together in his head she has climbed down from her stool and is walking away with the empty plate. He stands there watching her go. He can smell the zest of her orange, and good coffee, and an undernote of disinfectant.

Futh looks around, taking in the various bare tables and vacant chairs, the bar stools and the padded window seats, wondering where he should sit. There is a man standing behind the bar and Futh walks over to him. On the wall, there is an oversized clock. Futh did not see it last night when he arrived and he can't believe he missed it. It is enormous. The bar reeks of furniture polish and Futh detects a note of camphor. The man has his hands flat on the bar, his fingers splayed, his manicured nails like the display of eyes on a peacock's tail. He is well-dressed, although there is a fly, Futh notices, on the collar of his shirt. Futh recognises him as the man he saw in the corridor the night before. He took him for another guest but clearly he is a member of the hotel staff. Futh, speaking carefully in German, asks about breakfast.

Bernard shakes his head.

'What time is breakfast?' persists Futh.

Bernard looks him silently in the eye for a moment and says, 'You should go.'

Futh does not understand. He is not certain what the man has just said, does not know his tenses. He thinks he might know what was said but it makes no sense. He has paid the bed and breakfast rate but there appears to be some problem which he can't comprehend. He tries again to get an answer to his query, but the man only stares at him, saying nothing more.

Futh gives up, returns to his room and packs.

His suitcase will be collected from his room after he has left. It will – unless there is some problem with this service too – be taken to the next hotel on his circuit and be waiting for him when he arrives this afternoon.

Although good weather is forecast, Futh packs his waterproofs in his rucksack. He has maps and a compass, a guidebook and an English-German dictionary; he has drinks and snacks; he has a spare pair of walking socks and first-aid supplies; he even has cutlery and an emergency sewing kit. He already has his silver lighthouse in his pocket and can think of nothing else he needs. At the last moment, he remembers his book which is still lying on the bedside table underneath the lamp. Fetching it, he finds, lying on the cover, last night's moth.

He puts his rucksack on his back and begins to leave the room but, having lost out on breakfast, does not make it past the coffee-making facilities. He fills the kettle from the bathroom tap and, while he is waiting for the kettle to boil, empties the sachet of coffee granules and the little pot of UHT milk into a cup. He thinks about Carl's mother, about the breakfast she might have made for Carl, with cafetiere coffee and home baking. He wonders if he might have made a mistake.

The kettle boils. He fills up his cup and brings his coffee briefly to his lips, testing its heat, before setting it down on the windowsill to cool. He puts the packet of complimentary biscuits in his pocket and then idly checks inside the drawers and the wardrobe. He does not recall putting anything in them – he has not unpacked – but, he thinks, he always manages to leave something behind. Invariably, he overlooks a coat still hanging in a wardrobe, his passport at the back of a drawer or in the pocket of the coat in the wardrobe, pyjamas tangled up in the bedding, something plugged into the wall, or a toothbrush, countless toothbrushes, although they are easy to replace.

Getting down on his knees, he looks under the bed, just in case he has lost anything under there. There is something unidentifiable right in the middle. He reaches under and fishes it out. It is soft, some small piece of balled-up clothing, covered in dust and fluff and stray pillow feathers. Standing, shaking out and dusting off and looking at what he has retrieved, he finds in his hand a pair of knickers. He wonders how long they have been there.

Remembering his coffee, he turns back to the window and picks up his cup. While he drinks, he watches the few people now passing in the street below. He thinks about all the dust which he has just shaken from the knickers now being in the air which he is breathing, and most of that dust, he thinks, is strangers' dead skin.

He finishes his coffee, puts the empty cup back by the kettle and leaves the room.

In the lift, he realises that he is still holding the knickers. They are clenched in his closed hand, slivers of pink satin showing between his fingers. He does not know what to do with them, who to give them to. Entering the bar, he hesitates before putting them down – very carefully, as if they were fragile – on the landlady's check-in desk, next to her ledger. Embarrassed, glancing around, he finds himself observed by the barman who refused him breakfast.

Futh, making his way to the door to the street and stepping out into the sunshine, is aware of the barman watching him go.

The east-facing frontage of the hotel is bathed in sunlight. Walking away, turning back to see, he has to squint, it is so bright.

He walks alongside the Rhine to the ferry point. Waiting on the slip for the boat to come across from the far side, he takes his packet of biscuits out of his pocket and eats one. He is bewildered by the lack of breakfast, and by the man behind the bar who said, 'You should go.'

The little ferry arrives and Futh embarks. He leans against the side and eats the other biscuit, gazing back at Hellhaus and its backdrop of green hills and rocky outcrops.

The boat pulls away from the shore and the broad, grey-green river flows fast around and beneath it.

Futh, who is wearing shorts for the first time in years, takes the sun cream out of his rucksack and applies it to the exposed parts of his white legs, his forearms, the small triangle of bare chest where he has left his top two buttons undone. The crossing is short and he has barely finished rubbing the cream into the back of his neck before they reach the other side.

Futh sets off, following his printed directions, walking briskly, relishing the exercise, the doing of something physical, enjoying the clean, fresh air and the sound of twigs cracking beneath his feet. He follows his route along the river, which curves initially towards the west. He walks with the heat of the sun on his back, his hiking boots gathering dust from the dry path.

His last pair of hiking boots was bought especially for the trip he took with his father. The two of them were not used to hiking together. He had never seen his father wearing hiking boots before. Futh's boots were a bit big, even with two pairs of thick socks, as if they were expected to last for many years, but he probably never wore them again and has not had another pair until now.

These new boots are only a few days old. The lady in the shop said, 'Wear them in at home first, just around the house, and then take them out for little walks, building up the distance gradually.' But Futh did not do that. He packed them in his suitcase with the price tag still attached.

'You have to be careful,' his father had said, as they picked their way slowly down a steep embankment, 'of women, or before you know it you're married, and there are children, and then you're ruined.'

Twelve-year-old Futh, on the slope, trying to descend steadily, held on to the grass and low branches and found that they came away in his hands, coming with him as he stumbled and slid to the bottom.

'We can do without her,' his father said as they walked on. But Futh knew that every woman his father brought into the hotel room was a substitute for her. Some of them even looked like her. And Futh, seeing the women going into the bathroom, watching them in the mirror in the middle of the night, desired them himself.

It would be some years before Futh went to bed with a girl, and more before he met Angela, and even then it was often these women he found himself thinking about as he came.

He met Angela at a motorway service station. It was a Sunday and he had been to his father's place for lunch. His father had, by then, moved out of his sister's house and into a flat. It was less than an hour's drive down the motorway from where Futh lived, but at the time Futh still could not drive. He had hitchhiked there, and then his father had driven him half the way back, dropping him off at the service station so that Futh could find someone else to take him the rest of the way home.

Futh got himself a cup of coffee from a vending machine and then stood outside, beside the slip road, with his thumb out, waiting for a lift. It was not late but it was winter and already getting dark, and it was raining. Vehicle after vehicle drove by while the rain got heavier, but finally a little car slowed and stopped just past him. He hurried to the passenger door and looked in through the window. The driver had put the light on and was leaning across the seat to open the door, but Futh did not yet recognise her.

'How far are you going?' she asked. He told her and she said, 'That's not far from me. I can drop you there.' With relief, Futh clambered in and closed the door.

He was aware of the smell of his own rain-wet coat mixing with the smell of cigarette smoke which filled the inside of her car. Futh did not smoke himself but sometimes he found the smell of cigarette smoke almost painfully pleasant.

She said, 'My name's Angela.'

'That's my mother's name,' said Futh, buckling up.

Angela switched off the light, turned the blower on the misting windscreen and set off. While she negotiated her way onto the dark motorway, Futh was looking at her closely, struck by something about her which seemed familiar, trying to think what it was.

His wet hair was dripping onto his face and down the back of his neck. Spotting a towel in the footwell, he reached for it, saying, 'Do you mind if I . . .' and when she looked, opening her mouth to reply, he was already using it, rubbing his face and his hair and the back of his neck and his throat with it.

As she turned away again, he realised where he knew her from. On his first day of secondary school, he had developed a crush on a girl in his year. She had never noticed him and they had never spoken, except for the very first time he saw her, when he got in her way on the stairs and she said, pushing past him, 'Fuck' or 'Fucking' something. With her irritated face an inch or two from his, she had looked right at him and said through lightly glossed lips, 'Fuck' or 'Fucking'. He had noted the incident in his diary along with her sugary scent. She had not been in any of his classes but he used to catch sight of her at the school gates, in assembly, in the corridor, and sometimes – through a classroom window – on the sports field.

He had discovered her first name. Sometimes he walked home behind her, mentally composing his diary entry for the evening: *Angela was wearing a red jumper and a grey skirt and had her hair in a ponytail.* Or, *Angela was wearing a white blouse and grey trousers and her hair was shorter.*

Kenny – who had always had girlfriends, sometimes more than one at a time, even in junior school – would have whistled to make her look round, to make her smile or at least notice him. He would have spoken to her, made her laugh. But Futh was not Kenny. He kept her in sight but kept his distance, as if he were a private eye. He was so focused on her, blinkered, that he did not pay attention to where he was going. When Angela disappeared into her house, he stopped and looked around, finding himself on a strange estate, wondering where he was. Keen to get back and update his diary, he turned around and tried to retrace his steps, succeeding only in straying further and wishing he had gone straight home from school.

In the sixth form, Futh attended an open day in the Faculty of Science and Engineering at the local university. He was in the lecture theatre, gazing at the back of Angela's neck instead of at the person giving the welcome and introduction, when a movement beside him caught his eye. Turning, he found Kenny sitting down next to him. Kenny, whom Futh had not seen for years, had changed in some ways – he had a chipped front tooth and a stud in his nose;

he said that he had pierced it himself. But in other ways he was just the same – he had a bit of a gut, and bike oil on his hands.

'So there you are,' said Kenny, as if Futh were the one who had gone away. 'My mum said you'd be here. And she said you've got my old compass. Do you know her?' Futh was confused and then realised that Kenny had seen him staring at Angela. He sensed that he was about to be teased.

'I know her from school,' said Futh.

Now Kenny was looking at her too. Angela, as if she had a feeling that she was being observed, turned around and saw Kenny watching her while Futh glanced away.

The welcome came to an end and everyone left the lecture theatre and gathered in the foyer in little groups. Futh saw Angela leaving her friends and coming over. Standing next to Futh, looking at Kenny, she said, 'Do I know you?'

'He knows you,' said Kenny, indicating Futh.

Angela glanced at Futh and then turned back to Kenny and said, 'I don't know him.'

'We go to the same school,' said Futh.

'Do we?' said Angela.

Futh nodded. 'We're in the same year.'

'I don't recognise you,' she said.

This wasn't surprising, thought Futh. Shortly afterwards, Angela wandered away and Futh looked down at his schedule to see what he should do next. Kenny said, 'You can keep my compass. I got a new one anyway,' and when Futh looked up again he found that Kenny had drifted off too.

Kenny did not in the end go to university, and when Futh started his chemistry course that autumn, he discovered that Angela was not there either. He did not see her again until she picked him up at the motorway service station.

In the car, he reminded her of their encounter at the open day.

'I don't remember,' she said.

'Do you remember me from school?' he asked.

'No,' said Angela.

'We were in the same year.'

'I don't remember you,' she said.

'You might remember my dad,' he said, 'Mr Futh, the chemistry teacher.'

But no, she said, shaking her head, she did not remember him either.

'He's retired now anyway.'

By now the rain was falling so heavily that Futh could barely see where they were going. Angela, squinting through the windscreen, speeded up the wipers and turned up the blower. She was going a bit too fast for Futh's liking.

He asked her, 'Have you been away for the weekend? Have you come far?'

'No,' she said, 'I just drove out to the service station to meet my boyfriend.' After a moment, she added, 'It's in between his house and mine. We meet in the middle. He's married so we can't meet at his, and I live with my mother and she doesn't like me seeing him so we can't go there.'

They drove for about a mile without either of them

speaking and then Angela pulled over and stopped on the hard shoulder and Futh realised that she was crying. She was doing it rather quietly and he wondered when that had started. He did not know what to do. He said, 'Are you all right?'

She kept trying to talk but Futh could not understand her because she was crying at the same time. There were no tissues in the car, but there was the towel, although it was a bit damp. He offered it to her and she hesitated briefly before taking it and pressing her face into it and crying harder.

Futh watched the windscreen – the wipers struggling to keep up with the hammering rain – and eventually she said, 'I think he's seeing someone else.' When Futh said nothing for a moment she added, 'I don't mean his wife. I mean, I don't think I'm the only other one. I'm just waiting for him to turn around one day and say he's done with me.'

Futh sat awkwardly beside her. Kenny, he thought, would do the right thing. Kenny would put his arm around her, say something which helped. But what, he thought, did one say? *It's going to be fine. Maybe it's for the best. You'll find someone else.* But Futh was not Kenny.

After a minute, Futh looked in his bag and found a packet of mints which he opened and offered to her. She shook her head without really looking. He went back into his bag and found an orange and offered her that. She looked at the orange and then at him and she laughed. 'Go on then,' she said.

Futh peeled the orange and Angela took the half he passed to her and she said, 'You know, I do remember Mr

Futh. He was OK,' and she put an orange segment in her mouth. 'A bit boring,' she added.

When the orange was all gone, Futh wiped his fingers on the towel and Angela started the car again and they went on their way.

As they approached a junction, Angela began to indicate and Futh said, 'It's the next one.'

'There's been an accident there,' said Angela. 'If we go that way we'll be stuck in a jam for hours. I'm taking the back roads.'

They took the back roads, but later, after she had dropped him off and driven away, Futh, sitting alone at his kitchen table, wished that they had taken the other route, longed for the traffic jam in which he would still be sitting with Angela in her small, warm car.

After a few hours of walking, Futh's new boots begin to rub. The same thing happened on the trip with his father, who sat down at the end of the first day and said, 'I'm done in. No more walking,' and Futh had not complained. Instead, apart from one day spent visiting, they spent the rest of the week killing time until, at the end of each day, Futh's father went out and Futh went to bed, earlier every evening.

Futh, sitting down now on a bench, the hot slats griddling the backs of his thighs, reaches into his rucksack for a drink and finds that he has already finished what he brought. At the same time, it occurs to him that he has neglected to put any sun cream on his face, and that he ought to be wearing a hat. He administers some factor fifty, smearing it over the scalp exposed by his thinning hair, his skin already salmon pink and tender. Rubbing the residue into his hands, he sees on his palm the inch-long scar, now thin and pale.

He got the scar in Cornwall. He was up on the cliffs with his parents. It was the start of the holidays, the summer between primary and secondary school, the summer of the heatwave. They were spending the week in a caravan and someone had told them that the way to stop it turning into an oven was to keep the windows closed and the blinds down. They would come out of the midday sun into the relative cool of the darkened caravan and then there might be lunch and a siesta before Futh could escape again into the blazing day.

Despite the incredible heat, up on the cliffs there was a breeze and one could burn unexpectedly. They had eaten a picnic. His mother had made sandwiches and he and his father had shared a savoury pasty in a paper bag. His father had opened a bottle of Pomagne but no one else wanted any. There were oranges but only his mother had bothered with one. Afterwards, she lay on her back on the grass and closed her eyes. Her port-wine stain was visible beneath the strap of her bikini top. She smelt of sun cream.

His father was holding forth on the subject of the light-house and eighteenth-century shipwrecks. 'Of course,' his father said, 'there were still shipwrecks after the lighthouse was built.' He talked about the plundering of the wrecks, and the bodies which were washed ashore and buried, he said, until the early nineteenth century, namelessly in the dunes, in unconsecrated land.

He talked about flash patterns. 'The light,' he said, gazing fixedly at the hazy horizon, 'flashes every three seconds and can be seen from thirty miles away. In fog, the foghorn is used.' And Futh, looking at the lighthouse, wondered how this could happen – how there could be this constant warning of danger, the taking of all these precautions, and yet still there was all this wreckage.

His father went on.

Futh, standing, stretching his legs, wandered away over the bone-dry grass, searching for shade although there was none, hoping for more of a breeze, and wanting just to keep moving. In his hand was his mother's perfume case, a silver-plated lighthouse, which he had taken out of her handbag. It was an antique, an heirloom acquired from his father's German grandmother.

Futh took the glass vial out of its case. He wanted to smell the contents, his mother's scent, but he was not allowed to remove the stopper.

He remembered the visit to his widower granddad's flat in London, during which the lighthouse had been given to Futh's father. The whole time they were there, his granddad had been toying with it, this little silver novelty, occasionally putting it away in the pocket of his pyjama top only to get it straight out again. He seemed to be dwelling on something. Finally he said, 'You've never met Ernst, my brother, have you?' He was speaking really to his son.

'No,' said Futh's father, 'I haven't.'

'He might still be alive, I suppose.'

'He could be.'

Futh's granddad held out his hand, this exquisite silver

lighthouse lying across his palm. 'This was my mother's,' he said. 'You need to return it to Ernst.' He held it out until Futh's father took it from him, and then, seeming exhausted, Futh's granddad closed his eyes.

Outside, in the car, Futh's father gave the lighthouse to Futh's mother, who admired the case and the vial inside, approved the scent and put some on her wrists and her throat. The car, not yet out of sight of the house, filled with the smell of violets.

Futh, up on the cliffs in Cornwall with the silver lighthouse in one hand and the stoppered glass vial in the other, wandered back to his parents. His mother was still lying with her eyes closed, her face turned to the sun. His father was looking out to sea and then Futh heard him say, 'The foghorn blasts every thirty seconds.'

'Do you know,' said his mother, 'how much you bore me?'

There was a pause and then his father quietly packed away the picnic. Snapping shut the cool-box lid, he stood and looked at his wife. Futh watched the gulls fighting over the remains of their lunch, and then he looked down at his hand and saw the glass vial broken in his palm, the fleshy pad beneath his thumb cut open. The volatile contents of the lighthouse soaked into his wound, stinging, and ran between his fingers, soaking his boots, and the scent of it rose from him like millions of tiny balloons escaping towards the sky.

For a long time afterwards, he would lift the palm of his hand to his nose, searching for that scent of violets.

He wakes on the bench with his chin on his chest, his neck aching as he lifts his head and looks around him. He stares for a while at the cloudless sky and then checks his watch and consults the route details and the map. Finally getting to his feet, he presses on towards a village. He is fiercely thirsty.

The outlying houses are quiet. He pictures couples and families inside eating lunch together or slumbering afterwards while they wait for the heat of the day to subside. He envies them their dinners, their sofas, their cool interiors. He thinks about knocking on a door and asking for a glass of water, imagines being invited to step inside and sit down at a table on which lunch is still out. He chooses a garden gate which has been left ajar. He walks up the path to the door and knocks and waits, but nobody answers.

Just beyond the houses is a shop, through whose windows he can see refrigerated drinks for sale. But the door is locked and there is no one behind the counter, and the sign on the door, he realises, says 'CLOSED'.

Further along, there is a pub, which is open, or at least the door is. He wanders inside. There is nobody in the place – no customers at the tables, no one behind the bar. There are drinks behind the bar – pumps full of cool beer, fridges full of cold bottles, ice buckets with chilled wine bottles in them. He stands there looking at the drinks he wants, calling out, 'Hello?' He calls in both English and German, 'Hello? Hello?' But nobody hears him, or at least they don't come. He considers helping himself, leaving some money, but when he gets closer he sees that there is a dog in between himself and the bar, a big dog which Futh had not noticed at first, or perhaps he had, perhaps he just thought it was something else, a rug. The dog opens one eye.

Futh leaves, going back out into the street, into the sun, walking on past the houses, and there is a man, he sees now, one man labouring in his garden. Futh stops and asks him for a glass of water. The man, seeing the map in Futh's hand, asks him in English where he has come from and where he is going. Futh opens out his map and shows him. 'Well,' says the man, 'you're going in the right direction.' Futh's finger continues up and up on one side of the Rhine, and then, crossing the river, it slides back down over the squares of the map, to Hellhaus.

'You're staying at the hotel?' asks the man.

Futh says that he is. 'It's all right,' he adds, 'although my bedroom wasn't entirely clean, and the bathroom was a bit poky, and I didn't get my breakfast.'

'Stay here,' says the man. He takes off his gardening gloves and disappears into his house, coming out again with a child's plastic cup half-full of tepid water which he hands to Futh. Futh drinks it and thanks the man, lingers a little longer and then walks on.

In the middle of the afternoon, the heat begins to give a little. Futh, with his route details in his hand, pauses for a view of the river at its narrowest and deepest point where the currents are strong, looking for the siren, a vast nude cast in bronze. It is only then, when he is standing still, that he notices how much his feet hurt.

He takes the last mile slowly. Reaching the town and that night's hotel, he sits down on the doorstep to unlace his dusty boots. As he eases them off his feet, the smell of hot socks escapes like a groan. Underneath the bloodied wool, his heels are tender, his smaller toes too.

He goes inside, finds the owner and is given the key to his room which is on the ground floor with French windows overlooking a little rose garden. He limps into the bathroom and washes his feet in the sink, dabbing at the sore bits with a sponge. There is an inviting bath but he is too tired. He puts on his pyjamas and gets into bed, not even trying to read, just turning off the light.

Another thing which he knows always irritated Angela was the look on his face whenever she came home smelling of cigarette smoke. In the early days, he had not objected in the slightest when he thought that Angela had been smoking. He even liked the smell. But by the time they began trying for a baby, he did indeed mind when she came home smelling of cigarettes, when Angela – who claimed not to smoke and who would always mention a stinky staff room or some pub she had been to or a friend who had smoked in her car – tasted of smoke when he kissed her. He wished that she would at least suck mints before coming home to him. He noticed it more towards the end of their marriage. He supposed that she was unhappy and this was her crutch.

And their trying for a baby was a source of tension in itself. There were many pregnancies but each time she lost the child. She accused him, in each aftermath, of rushing her into another attempt, however much time had gone by. He reminded her of her age. 'Time is running out,' he said to her. She was thirty when they met but forty-four when she became pregnant for the final time, some months before they separated.

He turns onto one side and then the other, worrying about intruders hiding in the garden, behind the rose bushes, coming in through the French windows while he is asleep. He wonders how fast he could run. He is already regretting not having that bath. He can feel his muscles stiffening.

CHAPTER SIX

STILETTOS

Just after noon, on the day after the storm, Ester lets herself into the private apartment. Despite Bernard's warnings, Ester has left the door unlocked again. Sometimes Bernard discovers the unsecured apartment and gives her a lecture, a reminder. 'It's an open invitation,' he says.

Inside, Ester finds that she has also left the lights on. This is another bad habit of hers, turning on the light when she enters a room and then forgetting to turn it off when she leaves so that sometimes the whole of Hellhaus is ablaze.

She has finished her work for the day. The rooms are as clean as they are going to be and she is not expecting any guests this afternoon.

In the bedroom, she sits down at the dressing table and looks in the mirror. She sees the little creases at the corners of her eyes and mouth where her make-up has gathered; her short-cut, home-bleached hair grown out, the shape gone and inches of dark roots showing. Her gold-effect necklace burrows into her shallow cleavage, and the denim bulge of her stomach rests on her spreading thighs like a warm cat comfortably settled in her lap.

She was impressive as a girl. She remembers the look on Bernard's face the first time he laid eyes on her. She was twenty-one, with platinum blond hair in a pixie cut. She was slender and shapely, her figure flattered by the pink satin dress she was wearing for her engagement party. The dress was sleeveless and backless, the hemline just above the knee.

She was in her stilettos phase and had a collection of high heels in black and white and silver and pink and all sorts. She kept them in their boxes with Polaroids of the empty shoes stuck to the front. But when she met Bernard, she was wearing his mother's slippers.

Ida had welcomed Ester into the family the moment Conrad brought her home. She called Ester her daughter-in-law long before Ester and Conrad became engaged. When Ester visited, she spent most of the time in Ida's kitchen, helping her with the cooking. It was a standing joke that Ida saw more of Ester than Conrad did.

Being in Ida's kitchen reminded Ester of cooking with Lotte, the au pair she'd had as a child while her mother was away from home, travelling for the toiletries company. Ester had been very fond of Lotte and some of her favourite memories were of being in the kitchen while Lotte was cooking, being given jobs to do such as peeling potatoes and greasing baking trays.

Ester was no cook really, but she did like being in Ida's kitchen, being Ida's assistant, and while they worked, they talked.

Ida told Ester about the off-the-rails boy she had dated before meeting the man she had married, Conrad and Bernard's father, and Ester told Ida about a married man with whom she had been involved before Conrad. Ida told Ester how scared she had been when she first discovered she was pregnant with Bernard, when she was not yet married to his father, and Ester told Ida that she had been pregnant once, when she was with the married man, and that she had been very scared and had not in the end been able to go through with it.

'Is that dreadful?' she said to Ida who stood quietly stirring the gravy.

'You were young,' said Ida.

'I don't know,' said Ester, 'if I want children at all.'

'You're still young,' said Ida, turning off the gas and emptying the saucepan into the gravy boat and carrying it through to the dining room where the men were waiting.

On the day of the engagement party, while Conrad was getting drunk in the living room, Ester was in the kitchen with Ida, icing buns with an apron on and her high heels off, a spare pair of Ida's slippers on her feet, when the doorbell rang. A delivery of flowers was expected, arrangements of pink roses for the party. Ester, dusting off her icing-sugared hands, said, 'I'll get that.'

Walking towards the front door, she saw the figure of a man through the patterned glass, the sun behind him. She had never met Bernard, Conrad's older brother, who did not live nearby and rarely visited, but when she opened the door she recognised the eyes which gazed at her, taking her in, and the mouth which smiled and licked its lips, and even something in the voice which said, 'You must be Ester.' She knew without needing to ask that this was Bernard, who moved towards her and then past her and stood in the hallway removing his coat and his shoes, while Ester stood holding on to the open door, the sun coming in.

She could have sworn that it happened for both of them at that same moment. When, much later, he said that it had not happened for him until after that, it was like her having heard a fire engine or an ambulance going by as he stood there on the doorstep, and Bernard claiming to have heard it perhaps hours later when he and she and everyone else were outside on the patio. It had happened for him, said Bernard, while he was looking at her calves, slim and sleek between the hem of her dress and the ankle straps of her stilettos.

Before the end of Bernard's visit, Ester had taken up with him and broken off her engagement to Conrad. The first time Bernard came back to see her, they met at Ida's house. Everyone, said Bernard, letting her in, was out for the day. As he no longer lived at home, and slept, when he was there, on a sofa bed in the living room, he suggested that they go into Conrad's bedroom, but Ester did not want to. Bernard was less keen on using his parents' bed but in the end he settled for that. Afterwards, while Bernard was in the shower, Ester stood looking through the things on Ida's dressing table, admiring a hairbrush inlaid with mother-of-pearl. Hearing the front door slam, she dressed quickly and picked up her handbag, ready to go. But she was not sure what to do and stood for a while on this side of the bedroom door. Hearing nothing, she opened the door and went to the top of the stairs, and at that moment Bernard came out of the bathroom with a towel around his waist, and Conrad came up the stairs. She would not have minded a scene, but Conrad just looked at her and at Bernard and went without speaking into his room and that was unbearable.

Ester did meet Bernard at Ida's house again, but she did not go in. Ester remembers Ida opening the front door, turning away to call for Bernard and then turning back and looking silently at Ester until Bernard appeared in the hallway and took Ester away. Ida did not say, 'You've got a nerve coming here.' She did not say, 'You should be ashamed of yourself.' She did not say, 'The sight of you makes me sick.'

Even Bernard once said to Ester, 'What kind of woman does that?'

'It was you too,' she reminded him. 'He was your brother.'

'Well, I never liked him,' said Bernard, 'but he was your fiancé.'

Opening one of her dressing table drawers, Ester rummages through the jumbled contents, until, at the back, at the bottom, she finds what she is looking for – the perfume which Bernard gave to her as a wedding present. The case, like the one she found in the suitcase in room six, is designed to resemble a lighthouse, but this one is wooden, cylindrical rather than squared beneath the domed top, and less detailed than the silver one, but it does still have its vial of perfume inside. She takes it out. On one side of the glass vial, 'DRALLE' is written in relief. On the other side there is a sticker which says, 'Veilchen'. On the handle of the stopper there is an engraving of a dove, or a pigeon. She has not worn the perfume for years. She takes the stopper out of the bottle, puts it to her nose and smells the essence of violets.

Bernard married her quickly, as if he were afraid that she would change her mind, go back to his brother, or on to some other man. She went with him to the small town in which he was living. He liked, she was sure, to keep her far away from his brother and her old boyfriends and everyone she knew, as if loneliness were sure to keep her faithful.

Getting on for twenty years later, Bernard has aged well. He is a big man but he works out, lifts weights. He takes pride in his appearance. He is always well groomed. He smells of camphor, swearing by this essential oil which is, amongst other things, a disinfectant, a decongestant, an anaesthetic and a stimulant and which he adds to his bath-water every morning. He dresses nicely and wears polished shoes with segs in to make the soles and heels last, and his feet tippety-tap across the wooden floorboards.

She returns the perfume to her dressing table drawer and moves to the bed. Slipping off her shoes, she lies down on her side, sinks her head into the soft pillow and closes her eyes. Her breathing slows and her bare feet twitch as she falls quickly into sleep.

In her dreams, she hears the slow, teasing start of a tap dance, and when she wakes up there is a blanket over her, covering her exposed midriff and her bare legs.

CHAPTER SEVEN

STEWED APPLES

Futh sleeps badly before waking early, aching and sweating in twisted bedclothes. Getting stiffly out of bed, he finds a radiator blazing despite the hot weather. The small room is stifling. He turns the radiator off and tries to open the French windows but they are locked and there is no key. Taking off his damp pyjamas, he gets back into bed. He is unused to sleeping naked. He remembers how naked he felt the first time he went back to Angela's house and slept there without his pyjamas.

He had been in a bar. It was some months since he had seen Angela, since she had given him the lift home from the motorway service station. He had arrived at the bar with some people from work but they had all gone and he was alone with a woman. They were sitting on a very soft sofa which he found difficult to get out of. The soles of his shoes were stuck to the tacky floor. She was sitting close to him, this woman, leaning against him. She had syrupy gloss on her lips and glitter glue on her oily skin. Beneath the studs sparkling in her ear lobes, there were scars suggestive of earrings having been torn out.

'You're young,' she said. He was thirty. 'And you're not married? I usually meet married men.'

'No,' he said, finishing his drink and reaching forward to put the empty cocktail glass down on the glass table in front of them, 'I'm not married.'

'You need another drink,' she said.

Struggling to his feet, Futh went to fetch another round, but before he reached the bar he was surprised by the sight of Angela breaking away from a small group of people and crossing the room towards him.

'I know her,' she said when she reached him. 'You don't want to be with her. You don't want to be here.' She ushered him towards the exit and he went with her without asking any questions. They were almost at the door when it banged open and a small man darted in, glaring at Futh and Angela as he pushed past them. He made a beeline for the shiny, sticky woman sunk into the soft sofa on the far side of the room, kicking the glass table in front of her as he arrived, making the cocktail glasses jump, and shouting, 'Where is he? Where the fuck is he?' But Futh was already halfway through the door. The man began to harass bystanders, who backed away. The woman remained on the sofa sipping her drink and eating crisps.

Futh, outside on the pavement with Angela, his heart racing, said, 'My jacket's inside.' It was lying over the arm of the sofa. There was nothing in the pockets though – his wallet was in his hand – and it was not a cold night. He could still hear the small man shouting. He could hear things breaking.

'You'd better go,' said Angela.

'You'd better come with me,' said Futh as the fighting grew louder, moving closer.

'You could come back to my house,' said Angela.

Futh, remembering that Angela lived with her mother, said, 'I'd like that. I'd like to meet your mother.'

'She'll have taken her sleeping pill by now,' said Angela. 'She'll be out like a light until morning.'

People had started spilling out of the doors, escaping up and down the street, dispersing in pairs and groups, and Futh and Angela, moving on too now, looked like any other couple walking away.

He wakes again having dreamt about Angela. He knows that he should get up so as not to miss breakfast but he can't bring himself to move. He lies there naked and dozing and drifting back into his dream, and he is still there when he hears, through his semi-sleep, a knock at the door. He opens his eyes but he is not certain that the knock was at his door or whether there was a knock at all. After only a couple of seconds, he hears the door being unlocked, sees from his bed the door handle turning, the door opening, and then a maid standing in the doorway, stopped in her tracks. Futh raises himself up on his elbows and smiles at her. The maid says nothing but gives him a look which makes him shrink and then she leaves the room, pulling the door to behind her.

He gets up, washes at the sink and then dresses, putting

on his shorts and a clean short-sleeved shirt. He goes down to breakfast in his socks, with big plasters over his raw heels. The kitchen is closed but people are still finishing what is already out and Futh helps himself to the scraps. He eats some bread and cheese and pockets a hard-boiled egg in its shell for his lunch.

There are little vases of mixed flowers on each table, and he recognises, amongst other things, violets. He takes one out of his vase and puts it to his nose but he can't smell anything.

He planted violets in the garden when he and Angela first moved into their house. There was a huge bed of them and yet there was no scent at all.

'That's violets for you,' said Angela. 'You can't smell them.'

And so, to show her their scent, to demonstrate that you could smell them, he bought her a set of violet toiletries – bath oil, shampoo, soap, body lotion, eau de toilette. Angela looked at the gifts and said, 'I'm not your mother.'

At the table next to his, an attractive young woman is sitting alone. It occurs to Futh that at the time of that first trip to Germany, his father would have been about the same age as Futh is now. Futh can't imagine his newly single father – he can't imagine himself – in a hotel bar or some other bar or just in passing, starting up a conversation with a strange woman which would lead to his taking her back to his hotel room. What had his father said? *My son's asleep in the bedroom but there's a bathroom?* Futh imagined conducting a conversation with the young woman at the next table. How did one move so quickly from *Hello* to a hotel bathroom?

He has always courted women slowly, over months, starting with coffee in cafés and walks in the park, moving on to restaurants and art galleries and museums, not that it always got even that far. With Angela it was different. She was the one to take him to bed. After that first time at her mother's house, she came round to his place and when she arrived he took her coat and offered her a cup of tea and a scone and she rolled her eyes and said, 'I'm not your mother.'

Occasionally, and always in bed, she would talk about this married man who had been her boyfriend. 'He's always under a car or taking something apart,' she said after asking Futh whether he could look at her car, fix a headlight which wasn't working, and discovering that he could not. 'You're all in your head. He's more physical. Good with his hands.' She always talked about him in the present tense.

Futh, coming to the end of his breakfast and glancing again at the young woman sitting at the next table, finds that she has been joined by her rather large boyfriend. Futh finishes and leaves.

He eats his hard-boiled egg in the woods, enjoying the shade. He remembers his father carefully shattering the shell of a boiled egg while he talked about the powder, the egg substitute, which he had been fed as a child. 'It was OK,' he said. 'You make do.'

Futh had been anxious about spending a week with just his father, but, he had thought, how bad could a holiday be?

And as it turned out, in spite of the ferry and the women in the hotel bathroom and his father saying, 'We can do without her,' and things like that, Futh enjoyed their holiday. Futh – taking an egg from his father and holding it in his hand for a moment to admire its perfection before bringing it to his opening mouth – did not want it to end, did not want to have to go home ever again.

In the months between the decision that he and Angela would separate and his actually moving out, Futh had been visiting the parks and art galleries and museums which the two of them had never in fact been to, keeping out of her way. He visited the aviary, saw the exhibitions, sat in the cafés, and felt very much like his adolescent self on his climbing frame in the dark, putting off the moment when he would have to climb down and go in.

In the meantime, Angela was packing his belongings into self-assembly cardboard boxes, and each time he came home he found more of them stacked up in the spare room in which he had recently been sleeping.

'Come and keep me company,' Gloria had said, standing on the other side of the fence in her nightie. She had not brought out the rubbish this time, she had just come out and walked over to where he was sitting on his climbing frame, and Futh wondered how easily she could see him from inside her house. He had thought himself pretty much invisible sitting there in the dark. He wondered if she had noticed him watching her.

Futh tried to decline her invitation, but she lingered, leaning over the fence, cajoling him. Futh was also alone and he'd had no supper. He imagined Gloria putting something nice on the table just for him. Agreeing then to go with her, he climbed down and clambered over the fence, following Gloria over her lawn and into her house.

He sat on a bench at her kitchen table and watched her making drinks – putting ice in two glasses, adding something, a liqueur, which made the ice crack and shift. She brought the glasses to the table and handed him one, sitting down beside him, and Futh moved along the bench, into the corner. He took a sip of his drink and turned his face away towards the open window, through which he could clearly see his climbing frame looming over the little fence, the cloud-blurred moon above it.

On the window ledge, there was a Venus flytrap, its bright red leaves wide open. Gloria, sitting down, seeing him looking at her plant, said, 'It's a beauty, isn't it? Your daddy doesn't like it but I just love it. It catches every little thing that comes by.' Futh reached towards it, an outstretched finger poised to poke at a trap, to tickle its trigger hairs, to feel it close around him, and Gloria said, 'Don't do that.' He withdrew his hand, turning back to his drink, trying a little bit more, and Gloria said, 'It's caught a moth.' Futh looked. A trap had closed and there was something inside it, legs and the edges of wings poking out between the cilia. He wondered how it had managed that. He had not looked away for long. He was sorry to have missed it.

Years later, in his twenties, he would visit Japan, and he would see clingfilm-wrapped sea creatures in supermarket refrigerators slowly and uselessly moving their legs, and he would be reminded of the moth in the Venus flytrap in Gloria's kitchen.

'What happens now?' he asked.

'In a week or so,' said Gloria, 'the trap will open again. What's left will blow away.'

As Futh watched the moth struggling between the plant's tightly shut leaves, he felt a fingertip touching the back of his neck and the top of his back, underneath his T-shirt. 'You've caught the sun,' said Gloria. Futh stayed still, looking out at the darkness, feeling the slight weight of her touch on his skin, the warmth of her fingertip, and the line she had traced from the nape of his neck to the top of his spine, and then he heard her doing something on the far side of the kitchen and he realised that she was no longer touching him and probably had not been for a while.

Gloria was fetching more ice – returning to the table with the ice cubes already melting in her hand, water dripping between her fingers – and the bottle of whatever they were drinking. She encouraged Futh to finish the drink in front of him and then refreshed his glass. Sitting down again, she looked at him, cupped his face in her hands, and said, 'I can see your daddy in you.' From time to time, while they drank, she patted his knee or stroked his hair. When someone rang the doorbell, Futh jumped. Gloria stood and went to the front door.

Futh could not hear any voices. There was a porch with an internal door which Gloria had perhaps shut before opening the outer door. But he heard heavy footsteps going up the stairs. Gloria came back into the kitchen. 'You shouldn't be here,' she said to Futh. 'It's past your bedtime.' Leaving the kitchen again she said, without turning round, 'Let yourself out,' and she switched off the light as she went.

Futh felt a bit sick, like he did on ferries when the crazy carpet was seesawing under his feet. He stood up, holding on to the table, and then sat down again.

Some time later, he was still sitting there in the dark when he heard someone coming down the stairs, down the hallway, towards the kitchen. He expected to see Gloria coming through the doorway and was thrown when instead – smelling the pub before the light snapped on – he saw his father.

His father went to the fridge and took out a bottle of wine, and then opened the cupboard next to it and got out two glasses. Futh pressed his sunburnt back against the wall. His father, without noticing him, left the kitchen again.

Futh listened to his father's footsteps going up the stairs. He did not move when he heard the creaking of the floorboards overhead, and then the bedsprings, nor when he heard again the floorboards and then footsteps on the stairs and in the hallway.

The kitchen light snapped on again and there was his father going to a drawer by the sink and taking out a bottle opener. And then his father swung round to face Futh at the table, and for a long moment they just looked at one another. His father broke the silence. 'Go home,' he said. Futh waited, and his father came a little closer and said, 'Now.'

Futh stood up, slid along the bench and got himself to

the back door. As he stepped off Gloria's back doorstep, the kitchen light went out and he negotiated the plant pots and the bins in the dark. Climbing over the low fence into his own garden, coming down on the other side, he was sick into the empty flowerbed and onto the pitch-black grass.

His father has always made fun of him for not being able to hold his drink, as if he were not just the same. He ridiculed Futh for not knowing how to drive in his thirties, for still hitchhiking in his forties. When Futh finally took driving lessons and passed his test, his father criticised him for being the kind of driver who did not know the first thing about cars, for running out of petrol and for paying other men even to change a bulb in a headlight. And he mocked him for spending all day long trying to make paper smell like apples. 'What's the point of that?' his father said. 'You know you can buy actual apples?' Futh told him about the millions of tiny perfume bottles whose scent would still be there in twenty years. His father said, 'Real fucking apples. You can eat them.'

Futh's first memory is of playing under the kitchen table while his mother stewed apples for his dinner. She had the radio on and was humming along while she peeled and cored and chopped the apples and put the pieces in a simmering pan, and the kitchen was full of music and sunlight and the smell of unadulterated apple.

He recalls asking Angela, after they were married, if she could make an apple crumble. Finding her in the kitchen the next day cooking apples, he stood at her shoulder while she worked and he told her about this memory of his mother, how the smell of the apples took him back, and he saw her jaw tighten. The apple crumble came out well, but she did not make it again.

Futh, with sore feet and no need to hurry, arrives at his hotel in the late afternoon. He goes straight up to his room where his suitcase is waiting for him. After showering and taking a nap he goes out again, into the balmy evening, to look around the town before dinner.

Passing a pub with tables on the pavement, he stops and gets himself an unexpectedly huge glass of beer and watches the people walking by. The women his forty-something father brought back to the hotel were young, in their twenties perhaps. But Futh is not looking at the younger women, he is looking at those in their mid-thirties, the age his mother was when she left.

At the age of twelve, he wanted to go to New York as soon as he was old enough. In his twenties, when he could have travelled anywhere he wanted, he visited many cities and countries but he did not go to New York. He told himself that it was because he did not like flying – he generally went on coach tours – but he flew to Tokyo and Montréal. He did not go to New York until he met Angela, who wanted to go there herself.

On the aeroplane, during take-off, he began to imagine vividly there being a fire in the cabin or a terrorist amongst the passengers and being unable to escape. He felt the onset of the anxiety he always feels when flying, and he tried a relaxation technique which he had taught himself from a tape. He looked down at his feet, concentrating on them, breathing slowly and deeply, releasing all the tension in his toes, and in his arches, moving up to his ankles, still breathing slowly and deeply, relaxing his calves and then his knees, breathing slowly and deeply, his thighs . . . It was dark outside the aeroplane, and some of the passengers were switching off their overhead lights. He concentrated on his abdomen, and on his breathing, beginning to feel heavy, becoming drowsy, and, in the darkening cabin, falling asleep.

He dreamt that he had received a letter from his mother. She had written down her new name and address so that he would be able to find her, but however hard he looked at it he could not read her handwriting.

He opened his eyes with a desperate sense of something vital slipping away from him. Angela, sitting beside him watching a film, told him the new local time. Futh sat rewinding his watch, looking at the hands spinning backwards through the hours until even the date changed.

They went on a tour, on an open-top bus, although the top deck was full so they sat downstairs, people-watching through the windows. Stopped at traffic lights, Futh found himself staring at a woman who was looking in a shop window, whose face he could see reflected in the glass, a striking woman with greying blond hair. Quite slowly, as if she were an animal which might be startled, which might dart away, he got off the bus, approaching and touching her on the arm so that she turned around to look at him. He could not see her eyes through her sunglasses, or any port-wine stain beneath the high neckline of her dress, and she had not spoken before a man interrupted them, asking Futh what he wanted. When Futh failed to reply, the man took the woman's elbow and steered her away down the street. Futh watched them walking away, and after a while they paused again outside another shop and the man glanced back at Futh and the woman did too, and she took off her sunglasses, but she was too far away now for Futh to see her face clearly. But he had a feeling it was her.

He turned to look at Angela, to gesture through the window of the bus. He wanted to suggest, depending on the look on her face, that they abandon the tour and do the same thing, take a walk down the street, looking at the shop fronts. But Angela was not there. He watched the open-top bus picking up speed on the far side of the junction and disappearing into the distance with Angela on board.

'I really think it might have been her,' he said later, back at the hotel, walking down to dinner with Angela. 'I just had a feeling.'

'You said the same thing about the woman in Central Park,' she said. 'And you had a feeling about the woman in the deli.'

Futh and Angela walked into the hotel dining room, Futh with one hand in his pocket, his fingers wrapped tightly around the little silver lighthouse. He always took the lighthouse with him when he travelled, as if it were his Saint Christopher.

He took it to Germany when he went with his father. It was in his coat pocket when, having given up on the walking, they visited Futh's Great-Uncle Ernst. Futh had heard his granddad talking about his brother, asking

Futh's father to return to Ernst the silver lighthouse which
had been their mother's. Futh arrived at Ernst's house
with the lighthouse in his kagoul pocket, a secret inner
pocket – his father had one in which he kept the passports
and Deutschmarks, not trusting the hotel staff.

They did not actually know if Ernst was still alive. If he
was, he would be well into his eighties. Nor did they know
if he would have remained in his parents' house, or even
if the house was still standing. They did not make contact
before going. Their hotel was close enough for a day trip
and they went on spec, not really expecting to find Ernst
but going anyway, to see what was or was not there.

Arriving at lunchtime, they found the house standing
and clearly lived in, well maintained. The road was busy,
the only parking space some way from the house. Futh's
father knocked lightly on the front door and then stood
back. They waited for what seemed like a long time, noticing the twitching of a net curtain in an upstairs window.
They were on the point of turning away and leaving again
when the door was finally opened.

Futh was expecting his great-uncle to look like his
granddad. Futh had been eight when his granddad died
and only remembered him as an ill man, faded and
shrunken. But the man who stood in front of them was
unexpectedly large and solid.

'Ernst?' asked his father, and the man nodded. His
father spoke German – a greeting, an introduction – and
Ernst, although frowning, stepped away from the door,
inviting them inside.

Ernst took their coats, their matching kagouls, and

showed them to the living room which was up a flight of stairs. He shooed the cats off the chairs and went to fetch coffee, and a glass of milk for Futh. He was gone for quite a while, and the cats crept out from underneath the furniture, climbing back onto the chairs, settling themselves in the guests' laps.

Ernst returned, giving Futh his milk and pouring out the coffee and speaking with Futh's father in German. Futh could not follow the conversation, did not understand much of what was said until afterwards, on the journey home. When Ernst turned to Futh to tell him in German, 'You look like my brother did at your age,' Futh looked blank. Ernst said to Futh's father, 'Doesn't he speak German?' Futh's father said no, he did not. 'He should learn German,' said Ernst.

'It was your brother,' said Futh's father, 'who said we should come and see you.'

'Did he give you anything for me?' asked Ernst.

Futh's father took a swallow of coffee and said, 'No.'

Ernst shook his head. 'I doubt you know,' he said, 'the circumstances of his leaving home?'

Futh was looking around the room, taking an interest in the few small photographs displayed on the sideboard, which included one of himself. So, he thought, his granddad had written home, had at least sent pictures, and he was heartened by this because he supposed, therefore, that his mother might too. Looking, though, at the picture of himself, he felt that something was wrong, perhaps his hair. Then he realised his mistake – this was an old photograph, next to which there was a similar portrait of a little boy who was Ernst, and Futh understood that the boy in the first photograph was not himself but his young granddad.

'There was a girl,' said Ernst. 'There was always a girl, he ran from one to another. Well he got this girl into trouble. You know what I mean. He left because he thought he was going to get a beating from her brothers.'

The reason for his leaving was, apparently, no great surprise to his family. The surprise was his theft of his mother's few valuables. These, in fact, were returned by post soon afterwards, with the exception of a perfume bottle in a silver case.

'He must have given it,' said Ernst, 'to your mother.'

'Perhaps,' said Futh's father. 'But it was in my father's possession, intact, in his eighties. It was given to my wife.'

'It shouldn't have been,' said Ernst. 'That was my mother's, and mine to inherit. It has value. It ought to be returned.'

An insect crawled over the tabletop towards Ernst who, leaning forward, crushed it carefully with the back of his teaspoon, wiping the spoon on his trouser leg before using it to stir his sugared coffee.

'My wife and I are separated,' said Futh's father. 'I don't even have an address for her.' After a moment he added, 'The bottle got broken anyhow.'

Ernst sat back in his chair and looked at Futh, watched him drinking his full-fat, room-temperature milk. Futh, looking back at Ernst, was feeling a bit sick. Ernst, turning again to Futh's father, said, 'If it can't be returned, my brother should pay me for it.'

'I'm afraid your brother died,' said Futh's father, 'a few years ago.'

Ernst took a long look at Futh's father and then at Futh, perhaps considering whether someone else should be made to pay. He shook his head then and drank his coffee but every time Futh glanced up it seemed that Ernst was looking at him.

After a while, his father put down his empty coffee cup and said, 'Well, we should get going,' and he stood so that the cat fell from his lap. Futh, trying to do the same thing but doing it awkwardly, got scratched.

Ernst led the way down the stairs to the front door, on the back of which his visitors' kagouls were hanging on a hook. He took them down, handing the big one to Futh's father and the smaller one to Futh, who tried to take it, and Ernst, looking hard at him before letting go, said, 'You are just like my brother.'

Futh followed his father out onto the street, turning back to wave, to see whether he was still being watched. It seemed a very long way to the car, and the lighthouse, feeling huge now inside the little secret pocket of his kagoul, banged against his chest as he walked.

Futh finishes his second enormous beer and orders another. By the time that is gone, he is feeling pretty drunk. He stands up carefully and steps away from the table and into the street. He walks towards his hotel, trying to hum a tune which was a favourite of his mother's, but he can't get it. He concentrates on keeping his feet in the middle of the pavement, but every now and again his right shoulder scrapes against the wall, or the kerb falls away beneath his left foot.

Entering the hotel, he concentrates on walking in a straight line to the bar and then stands there swaying very slightly. There is a smell of damp dishcloths and dry-roasted peanuts which is making him feel ill. He sits down on a stool, thinking that he should have dinner.

He thinks of Angela sitting down to her dinner in their house, the house to which he will not be returning. When he gets back to England he will be moving straight into a flat. All those self-assembly boxes will be there, with all his things inside waiting to be unpacked. Angela will eat in what will now be her home and he will eat in his, and he wonders if they will still retain the habits of their marriage, sitting down to eat at the same time, having their main course at the table and their pudding on the sofa, watching the same television programmes while they eat. He imagines messaging her from his bedroom window – flash-flash-flash – before they each get into their separate beds and go to sleep.

There is a half-drunk beer in front of him. He does not remember buying it or speaking to anyone. He does not appear to have ordered food. He does not even have a menu. No one else is eating and the bar looks like it is closing. He stands up and goes to his room and it occurs to him that he forgot to pay for the beers he had in town.

He goes first to room six, before remembering where he is. Letting himself into his room, he thinks how much he would like a bedtime snack. He used to ask Angela, if he came home hungry after drinking, to make him a sandwich or something, and she used to say, 'I'm not your mother.'

He puts on his pyjamas and climbs into bed, wishing that there were someone who would bring him a little supper.

CHAPTER EIGHT

CHARMS

Ester has been lying awake for half an hour, watching Bernard sleeping beside her, watching him breathe. He is lying on his back with his face turned slightly away from her, but she sees his eyes open; she hears his breathing change as he wakes. Rolling onto his side, he reaches for his watch on the bedside table, looks at the time and sits up. Ester looks at his broad, naked back. She can feel the warmth of his body, the warmth in the sheets on his side of the bed; she can smell yesterday's camphor.

Bernard stands, walks over to the window and draws back the curtains, looking out at the fine morning. Only as he turns away from the window does he look back at the bed, at his wife who is lying there looking at him. He rubs his bleary face with both his hands and grunts by way of acknowledgement, and then he goes into the en suite bathroom and shuts the door. Ester stays where she is for a while, listening to the bathwater running and then hearing the sloshing and splashing as Bernard gets into the tub and begins his ablution.

She gets up and goes to her dressing table, sitting down and brushing her hair. Then, putting down the mother-of-pearl hairbrush and picking up her foundation, she begins to make up her face. She keeps her cosmetics in a drawer with her jewellery, most of which she never wears. Somewhere in amongst the tangle of chains there is a charm bracelet with half a dozen silver charms on it: a lucky horseshoe, a slingback shoe, an 'E', a '21', a snowflake, a love-heart.

On the day Ester and Bernard married, Ida endeavoured to find Ester alone, cornering her in the register office toilets. 'You are losing your sparkles,' she said, reaching out and savagely refixing Ester's diamante hair pins, the wire scraping along her scalp like rocks against the hull of a boat as it ran aground. Ida then lifted Ester's wrist, looking disparagingly at the bracelet she wore there, the charm bracelet which had been Ida's first Christmas present to Ester. The little collection of silver charms had been gifted on subsequent occasions, the fat love-heart the most recent present, given on her engagement to Conrad.

'You know,' Ida said, still holding Ester's arm as if she were weighing it, 'you are not the one Bernard loves.'

Ester, standing between the empty cubicles and the sinks, sweating into her wedding dress, her cheeks burning through her blusher, blinked.

'The only girl Bernard has ever loved,' said Ida, 'Conrad took and then rejected. This is just revenge.' A speck of saliva flew from Ida's mouth onto Ester's lower lip. When Ida released Ester's arm and left the toilets, Ester wiped her mouth and reapplied her lipstick, but still she felt it there, the fleck of spit. In the hours which followed, Ester put her mouth to the rims of countless champagne glasses and wine glasses and shot glasses, but still she felt that speck of saliva clinging on. And even hours later, when Ester and Bernard were alone in bed and he was kissing her, all she could think about was Ida's spit on her lip, as if it were still there, pressed between her mouth and Bernard's like a cold sore.

Bernard emerges in a cloud of camphor-scented steam, the bath draining noisily behind him. Ester chats to him while he dresses, watching him in the mirror as he chooses his clothes, inspects his nails, snaps his watch back onto his wrist, checks his shoes. He does not reply, and she does not say anything which requires a response, and he does not look at her.

After Bernard has gone downstairs, Ester gets dressed, putting on cleaning clothes, and goes into the bathroom. She rinses away the tidemark which Bernard has left in the still-warm tub. With a towel, she mops up the puddles on the floor, a patterned lino which she likes because it does not show the dirt. The wall tiles and the bathroom suite are white and show everything, every speck, but at least the tiles are porcelain, hardwearing.

She opens the bathroom cabinet and takes a cigarette and a lighter out of a box of tampons. She has a few little hiding places where Bernard, who does not like her smoking, will not look. Opening the window, she lights her cigarette and smokes it with the sun on her face, inspecting a Venus flytrap on the windowsill, talking to it. She finds the plant fascinating and sometimes pokes at the expectant leaves with the handle of her toothbrush, just to see them in action. Bernard does not really care for houseplants and finds the Venus flytrap vulgar, a little ugly.

She leaves the apartment and follows Bernard down to the bar to have breakfast with him. As she sits down, he asks her whether she has remembered to lock the apartment, and even as she tells him that she has, she knows that she has not.

They eat their breakfast and Bernard reads aloud from his paper when he finds something interesting, but he does not look at Ester as he does so.

Ester stays in the bar, the dining room, while the guests have their breakfast. The ones who are going check out, leaving her with their keys and their petty complaints. Then she cleans the first of the empty bedrooms, a family room downstairs. She could go up to the apartment and lock it now, but she does not. Before going upstairs, she allows herself a break, returning to the bar and sitting on her stool, having a drink. She watches Bernard working, although in between the breakfasters and the lunchtime crowd, it is relatively quiet. Even when there is no one to serve, he stays at the other end of the bar reading his paper.

At eleven o'clock, the new girl arrives, relieving Bernard, who goes off to do some other work. Ester goes upstairs to clean the remaining rooms. When she finishes, it is almost noon.

She and Bernard rarely eat lunch together. If Ester is hungry she has bar snacks, peanuts. Bernard likes to make his own lunch in their private kitchen upstairs. He has a thing about other people handling his food. When Ester returns to the bar, he is there, sitting at one of the tables, eating his meal. He does not look up when she comes in but when he has finished eating he walks over to her, leaving his plate behind on the table. He stops beside her and leans in front of her so that his arm is on the bar in between her and the drink she has fetched for herself. He puts his face very close to hers and tells her again about leaving the apartment unlocked. He says, 'You're asking for trouble.'

In the middle of the afternoon, when the new girl is on a break and Bernard is in the cellar and Ester is finishing off a drink, a tourist comes in. He approaches the bar close to where Ester is sitting. She does not find him attractive, but that is not important. Leaning towards him, she says, 'Buy me a drink.'

The man turns towards her and gives her a wary look.

Ester smiles at him and says, 'It's my birthday.'

He smiles back then, although he continues to look nervous. 'Well, sure,' he says. 'What would you like?'

Bernard, returning from the cellar, sees the man and comes over to serve him, and Ester says to the man, 'You're offering to buy me a drink?'

'Yes, I am,' says the man. 'What will you have?'

Bernard looks at his wife, although he is speaking to the man when he says, 'Is that right? You want to buy her a drink?'

Once more the man agrees to this. He looks in the fridges and at the pumps, choosing a beer for himself. 'And whatever the lady would like,' he adds.

Bernard, still staring at Ester, says, 'Get the fuck out.'

The man is confused. He laughs. Bernard, turning his head, looking directly at the man this time, repeats himself. The baffled customer backs away from the bar and leaves as quickly as he can.

Bernard resumes his position at the far end of the bar, picking up his paper again. Ester, who has no guests to wait for today, goes upstairs for a rest.

Sometimes she sleeps, and sometimes she just reads a book or a magazine, tearing out pictures of hairstyles she likes, tearing out party eyes and red mouths.

Later, when Ester goes to Bernard and says, 'I won't be here tomorrow lunchtime. I have an appointment,' he says, without looking up from his crossword puzzle, 'It makes no difference to me.'

CHAPTER NINE

ORANGES

Futh wakes in pain. His swollen brain is throbbing and the light hurts his eyes. He closes them and goes back to sleep. When he next stirs, it is late, mid-morning, and he has missed breakfast again.

He goes into the bathroom. Feeling fuzzy, holding on to the edge of the sink, he turns on a tap and splashes his face, his bed-warmed and sleep-steeped skin shocked by the cold water. He drinks straight from the tap, daring to touch the end of it with his lips despite the germs which his Aunt Frieda has told him flourish on taps and drinking fountains. Without looking at himself in the mirror, he returns to the bedroom. Going to the window and opening the curtains, he is pleased to discover a dreary morning, an overcast sky, the prospect of a cooler day.

He does not remember looking out of this window yesterday, either when he arrived or when he went to bed. He does not recall checking for an escape route. It is just as well, he thinks, because this room is on the third floor and there is nothing to climb out onto and nothing to break a fall. Had he realised this, he would have spent half the night worrying about it and the other half having bad dreams.

He sits down on the bed, next to his suitcase. It was his honeymoon suitcase, a wedding present from his father, who was his best man.

Futh had first asked a man at work, who turned him down. Gloria said, 'Aren't you going to ask Kenny?' So Futh asked Kenny, who just laughed.

Then he asked his father, who, shaking his head, said, 'Have you got no one else?' But he did it, and he took Futh out for a drink and said, raising his glass, that the French called this 'l'enterrement de vie de garçon'. 'The burial,' he said, 'of a boy's life.'

They held the wedding reception in the function room of a local pub. There was a dance floor on which his father slow-danced with Gloria, and onto which Angela's mother kept trying to persuade Futh, and which Angela repeatedly refused to leave despite Futh's preference for an early night. And there was a buffet which was drying out by the time Futh left Angela on the dance floor and went out into the corridor to get away from the disco's noise and flashing lights.

At the far end of the corridor, a back door was propped open and through it he could see one end of a patio in darkness and rain beginning to fall. He stepped outside and a security light came on, illuminating him on the empty slabs. There was a square of lawn, edged at his end by the patio and the wall to which the security light was attached. Running down one side of the lawn was the outside wall of the corridor, and on the opposite side a hedge screened the garden from the road. At the far end was the wall of the function room which he had just left, and above that the bedroom which he had booked for the night.

He wandered onto the wet grass. Rain always reminded him of meeting Angela at the motorway service station, the smell of his wet coat in her car. He ambled down to the end of the garden. He reckoned that if he stood anywhere else he could be seen from the function room, but standing against its wall he could not. And moreover, the security light sensor apparently did not reach that far. The light went off and Futh stood in darkness outside the function room, in thick grass between patches of nettles, enjoying the rain smell and remembering Angela.

'What you can smell,' he had said to her on some rainy woodland walk, inhaling deeply, 'is bacterial spores. They are stored in dried-out soil and released by rainfall and carried in the damp air to our noses.'

When Futh began to feel really wet, he headed back inside. As he crossed the lawn, the security light snapped on again and he felt like an animal in headlights, about to be mown down.

He did not go back into the function room but slipped past the open door and went straight upstairs to the bedroom. He heard the party continuing without him, and it sounded louder, he thought, than it had done when he was down there. He could hear the voices shrieking through the floorboards, feel the pulse of the disco music under his feet.

He went to the window and peered out, looking for his escape route. The room had a view of the lawn, and the patio on the far side. It was a dormer window – beneath it, the roof sloped away. Although he could not see down to the ground, he knew that if he had to jump he would land on grass, or at worst in the nettles near which he had been standing a few minutes earlier. Satisfied that he was safe, he drew the curtains.

He peeled off his damp clothes and hung them over the cold radiator and the backs of the chairs to dry. He took off his watch and put it down on the dressing table. Opening his new suitcase, he took out his wash bag and went to the bathroom. Angela's wash bag was already in there and he rummaged through it. He smelt a few of her products, and tested them, scrubbing his skin with her exfoliating cream in the shower. After towel drying himself, he trimmed his fingernails and toenails. He powdered his feet and put some of Angela's replenishing night cream on his face and neck, and balm on the thin skin around his eyes. He combed his hair and brushed and flossed his teeth.

Back in the bedroom, he looked through his suitcase for the outfit in which he would be going away, laying it out ready for the morning. He reassured himself that he had brought his wallet, the travellers cheques, the booking confirmation for the flight and the hire car and the honey-moon accommodation, lining all these things up next to his watch.

He put on his pyjamas, got into bed and switched off his lamp. He lay there, smelling of Angela, noting the total absence of light in the room – none coming in from outside, no little red dot from a television on stand-by, no digital

display of red or green numbers on a radio alarm clock –
and he waited for Angela to come up.

Some time later, he was woken by the security light
at the back of the pub flashing on, glaring through the
curtains. He got out of bed to look outside, reaching the
window and drawing aside the curtain just as the light went
off again. He stood in darkness, listening to the wedding
reception still going strong down below.

He opened the window, appreciating the cool night air.
He wondered whether there was anyone out there, in the
garden, but he could not see a thing – there was not much
light from the moon – and he could not hear anything due
to the noise from downstairs. He stood there for a while
looking out at the night, his duvet-warmed feet growing
cold on the bare floorboards, before he caught the smell
of cigarette smoke coming in through the open window.
After a minute, the security light snapped on again and he
saw Angela in her wedding dress, watched her crossing
the patio and disappearing through the back door. Antici-
pating her now coming to bed with the cigarette smell on
her skin and in her hair and in her mouth, he closed the
window and drew the curtain again.

He got back into bed, meaning to lie awake and wait for
Angela but instead falling asleep. He woke with no idea
what time it was or if Angela was with him. It was dark, and
it was quiet, the reception finally over. He reached across
to Angela's side of the bed, half-expecting to find it empty,
instead feeling the mound of her body beneath the covers,
touching her skin which was still cold from having been

outside. He whispered, 'Are you awake?' but she did not answer. He went back to sleep.

In the morning, they had breakfast in the dining room. Futh took a small continental breakfast from the buffet and went to sit at a table with his father and Gloria. He poured a cup of coffee for himself and one for Angela, but he did not start eating, preferring to wait for Angela who had wandered over to the cooked breakfasts. Turning to look for her, he saw her standing talking to Kenny. Angela, glancing up and seeing Futh watching her, made her way back to the table without a breakfast. Kenny turned back to the buffet, filling his plate.

'He'll be hungry,' said Gloria. 'He didn't get here until all the wedding food had been cleared away.'

'I didn't know he was coming,' said Futh.

'Of course he came,' said Gloria. 'He wouldn't have missed this for the world.'

Kenny came to the table and sat down with his full English breakfast. 'I don't get this at home,' he said, picking up his knife and fork.

'You would at my house,' said Gloria, but Kenny ignored her, cutting into his sausage and egg.

Futh began to say to Angela, 'This is Kenny,' but he was interrupted.

'They've already met,' said Gloria. 'They met last night.'

Futh said, 'They met before last night,' and Angela looked surprised. 'You met at the university open day,' he added.

Kenny, forking a piece of black pudding, wiping it in the spreading yolk of his egg, said, 'Do you remember that, Angela?'

She nodded, but gingerly, as if it hurt.

Futh said to Angela, 'I've known Kenny since infant school.'

'We were neighbours,' said Kenny. 'He pissed himself in my bed.'

Futh broke open his croissant and looked with annoyance at the way it fell apart, at the brittle, greasy flakes covering his fingers and his plate.

Angela seemed dazed. She pushed her black coffee away without drinking it, putting her forehead in the palm of her hand.

Futh looked up and said, 'You should have come to bed when I did.'

Angela, without taking her head out of her hand, said, 'Yes.'

When everyone had finished, Kenny took out his cigarettes and offered them around the table. When Angela declined, Futh, thinking that smoking was something she had learnt to do in secret, said, 'Have one.' He was more than happy for her to have the occasional cigarette. It would be months before he came to dislike the smell of it on her.

Looking confused, she said, 'I don't smoke.'

Kenny lit up and Futh excused himself, wanting to call the taxi company to make sure that the taxi was not going to be late.

When the taxi came, late after all, it was raining again. Futh held his coat over Angela's head as they hurried from the pub to the waiting taxi. They got in the back and Futh opened his window to smell the rain. After a few minutes of riding along like that, Angela leaned over and closed it and Futh caught a whiff of Kenny's cigarette smoke on her. He sat there in his damp coat looking out at all the rain and it was, he thought, a bit like the night he and Angela met at the motorway service station.

The honeymoon was dreadful – they had delayed flights and lost luggage, twin beds and upset stomachs, bad weather and arguments about Angela having to do all the driving, and then the hire car broke down.

'It was bad,' Angela told people afterwards. 'I'm not sure you could have a worse holiday.'

With the exception of their honeymoon, for which Futh was responsible, Angela took care of all their holidays. Even at Christmas, it was Angela who arranged for them to visit her mother, her father, his father, and Futh just went with her. Last Christmas, though, for the first time, they made separate arrangements and Futh went alone to his father's flat, which was really Gloria's flat, chosen for its proximity to Kenny and his family.

Futh drove over on Christmas morning. He had only been driving for a few months, had only ever driven to and from work, and never in the snow, which had fallen unexpectedly overnight. Angela had been picked up by her brother after breakfast and taken over to her father's house. Futh, leaving soon afterwards, found that his car refused to start in the cold weather, so he took Angela's. Searching for a scraper with which to clear the windscreen, looking in the glove compartment, he found a small towel.

He took it out and found it all crusted up. He sniffed it and put it back, clearing the windscreen with a credit card.

He could not see how to change the heater settings and a fierce jet of initially ice-cold and then increasingly hot air blew directly onto his toes as he drove up the empty motorway.

Gloria let him in with a smile. 'Come in out of the cold,' she said, taking the hat from his head before he was even through the door, slipping his coat off his shoulders, unwinding the scarf from around his neck. When the front door shut behind him, the hallway seemed very narrow; the space in which he stood, between the closed door and Gloria, seemed rather small. He felt naked without his outerwear on.

Gloria turned and led the way upstairs, her scent trailing behind her, and Futh followed.

In the living room, Gloria guided him past the dining table – already set with place mats, cutlery, wine glasses and crackers – to a seat on the sofa beside the roaring log fire. She filled a tumbler from a jug of mulled wine on the coffee table and pressed it into his hand. He took a few medicinal gulps of the piping hot wine and then leaned forward and put the glass down. Gloria topped up her own glass and sat down beside him, slipping off her mules and crossing her legs towards him, poking playfully at his leg with her big toe. He looked down at her bare foot, her hot-pink nail varnish.

'Your father's in a bad mood,' she said.

'Ah,' said Futh. 'Where is he?'

'He's in the kitchen.'

'I should go and say hello.' Futh leaned forward again, preparing to stand.

Gloria, putting her hand, her honeysuckle-pink finger-nails, on his thigh, said, 'No, you shouldn't.' Futh, after a pause, during which he picked up his glass again and took another scalding swig, settled back into his seat. Gloria's fingers plucked at his trouser leg, tugging at a loose thread. 'You've nobody looking after you,' she said.

Futh glanced at her. Firelight glinted off her oversized earrings. He looked away. Already he was feeling sedated by the mulled wine and the heat, pickled and roasted like his father's pork hocks. Once more he went to stand up, got to his feet and went to the window.

Outside, everything was buried under inches of snow. Futh leaned his forehead against the cool windowpane and watched a boy building an igloo in a back garden, the boy's breath visible in the cold air.

'Come back over here,' said Gloria. 'It's lovely and warm by the fire.'

Futh stayed where he was for a moment, gazing out, as if he had not heard her. Then, lifting his head and turning away from the window, he walked back to the sofa. He sat down where he had been and Gloria returned her painted fingertips to his thigh. She moved her face a fraction closer to his and said, 'You look so much like your father.'

'I'm not like him at all,' said Futh.

'You're more like your mother,' said Gloria.

Futh watched the fire blazing in the hearth.

'She left very suddenly, didn't she?' said Gloria. 'She just disappeared.'

'Yes,' said Futh, 'she did.'

There was a thud behind them and Futh looked up to see his father standing there with oven gloves on his hands, a roasted chicken on the dining table.

Gloria lifted her hand from Futh's leg and wrapped it around her glass. Standing, slipping her feet into her mules, she went to stand beside Futh's father, saying, 'That looks lovely,' but he was already walking away again.

He returned with a dish of vegetables and two bottles of wine. One bottle was almost empty and he poured the last inch into his glass, drinking half of it before raising the dregs to nobody in particular. 'To family,' he said.

Gloria sat herself down, straightening her cutlery and laying her napkin over her lap. Futh came over from the fire and took his place at the table. His father uncorked the other bottle of wine and emptied it into the three large glasses. He carved the chicken while Gloria dished out vegetables.

Futh took his plate and his father said, 'So Angola's leaving you.'

'We're separating,' said Futh, lifting his cutlery, 'yes.'

'What did you do?' asked his father.

'What?'

'Why's she leaving you?'

'I didn't do anything,' said Futh.

'She got bored,' said his father.

Gloria reached over and gave Futh's leg a consolatory pat and a squeeze.

Futh put down his cutlery and stood up. He was closer

to the window but went to the fire, crouching down in front of it and picking up the poker.

'Some women,' said Gloria, 'don't appreciate what they've got.'

Futh, stoking the still-raging fire, said quietly to himself, 'And some people don't know what's theirs and what's not.'

He did not hear his father moving from the table and crossing the room. He only knew someone was standing behind him when he was pulled up by his collar, turned around and smacked. He dropped the poker and it fell at his feet, its red-hot tip singeing the carpet. His father returned to the table. Futh picked up the poker, put it back where it belonged, followed his father back to the table and sat down.

They pulled their crackers and put on their paper hats. Gloria got a paste necklace in her cracker and wore that too, and they listened to the Christmas service on the radio.

After lunch, a rug was moved from another part of the room and placed in front of the hearth, covering the scorch mark made by the poker. 'There you are, you'd never know,' said Gloria, turning back the corner of the rug with her foot to take another look at the blackened carpet, poking at it with her bare toe.

His hangover is getting worse. Futh, drinking more water, wishes that he had thought to pack aspirin. He thinks about showering but just gets dressed instead, putting the lighthouse in his pocket and applying new plasters to his messed-up heels before pulling on his thick walking socks and, steeling himself, his boots. Then, zipping up his honeymoon suitcase and leaving it by the door ready for transfer, he sets off.

He walks two miles just looking for an open bakery. It is almost midday before he begins the day's hiking.

His route takes him across cornfields and then into forest. It is late August, almost autumn, harvest time, but for now the leaves are still green and there are blackberries on the bushes. The undergrowth is busy with mice and lizards and the air is full of darting insects nipping at him.

There are rain clouds gathering and the darkening sky and the forest canopy make it feel like dusk even in the early afternoon. Here and there, he emerges into daylight, coming to viewpoints overlooking the Rhine. It is possible to see a long way, to see miles of river and railway track, boats and trains on their way to Koblenz or Bonn, or further, to Cologne or Düsseldorf, or further still towards Rotterdam and Utrecht and the North Sea. But he is not looking, is unable to think of anything except how much his feet hurt.

When he rests, he feels his feet throbbing inside his boots. He knows that his plasters have come away, but if he takes off his boots he does not think he will ever put them back on. He continues on his way, the path returning him to the gloomy forest.

He walks ever more slowly as the afternoon wears on. The path seems never-ending but the viewpoints have tailed off. In the fading light, Futh, with everything but a torch in his backpack, begins to feel that the path might now be taking him deeper and deeper into the forest and that he might never find his way out. He could believe that the trees themselves were, in the darkness, shifting and spreading around him, to enclose him, to keep him there. He can barely see where he is treading, cannot tell what it is that his boots sink into here or what cracks beneath them there. At one point, he stops and considers turning back, remembering something he has read about deep-sea divers getting confused about which way is up, thinking that they are surfacing even as they dive deeper. But he ploughs on, and finally the trees thin out and he emerges from the forest into the twilight, returning to civilisation, and the streetlights are coming on to light his way.

He has passed the midpoint of his circular walk, has walked more miles than he has left to go. He will be back at his starting point, back in Hellhaus, by the end of the week, and every step now takes him closer.

He abandons the rest of the day's hiking. Finding his way to the station, he catches a train to his next overnight stop, resting his miserable feet and leaning his head on the rattling window against which the rain has begun to fall.

'There were still shipwrecks,' his father said, 'after the lighthouse was built.'

Futh's mother was sunbathing in a bikini top and shorts. She had taken off her walking boots and socks and stretched out her bare feet, but Futh still had his on. His father was wearing ordinary shoes and ruining them.

His mother liked to walk and Futh liked to go with her. There were hills where they lived, where the houses ended. You left the shop on the corner with your quarter pound of sweets in a paper bag and walked across a field and there you were, going up into the hills. The hills skirted the town. It was possible to walk for miles along the top without losing sight of their house, although his mother always kept walking until she did, humming tunes which were lost to the wind. His father never came, and his mother no longer asked him.

Up on the cliffs in Cornwall, his father was talking about wrecking and plundering, and telling some story about a ghost ship crashing over and over again into the rocks around the lighthouse, and Futh saw his mother rolling her eyes. He had seen this before, his mother fidgeting while his father held forth. This was how it always began, with his father going on in this manner and his mother rolling her eyes and twitching and sighing like some creature stirring. If, after some time, his father was still talking, his mother would begin with her provocative interjections. 'Nobody's listening,' she would say, or, 'Nobody cares.' And then perhaps there would be silence, or perhaps his father's temper would flare – he lost his temper easily but it was all over just as quickly.

She gave a great sigh. His father was oblivious. 'The light,' he said, 'flashes every three seconds and can be seen from thirty miles away. In fog, the foghorn is used.'

Futh wandered off, as if there might be somewhere to escape to. He had in his hand the perfume, the silver lighthouse, which he had taken out of his mother's handbag. Returning after a short while with the glass vial out of its silver case, he found his father still talking about foghorns, or perhaps he had been waiting and was just picking up where he had left off, and his mother said without opening her eyes, 'Do you know how much you bore me?'

Futh watched his father silently placing the remains of the picnic in the cool box, packing the plastic plates and beakers into the rucksack, putting the lid on the Thermos of cold coffee and shaking off the picnic blanket on which only he had been sitting, a breeze getting up as he tried to fold it. Finally, with everything packed away, his father stood still. He looked at his wife lying in the grass with the sun on her, and Futh watched the gulls. He watched them until his mother, standing, said, 'I'm going home,' and then, looking down, he saw his hand and the blood where he was cut, the little bottle broken, his mother's perfume in his wound.

The same afternoon, they collected their luggage from the caravan site and took the train back from Cornwall. His mother changed in the toilets, swapping her sun clothes for travelling clothes and putting on shoes with heels, slipping them off again as soon as she sat down.

When the train was moving, his father went to the buffet car and did not return until they were almost home. His mother fell asleep with her bare feet on the grubby floor, her short, pale-blond hair resting against the dirty window. The perfume case, containing the broken glass vial, was in Futh's pocket. She might have known he had it, but did not ask for it back. His unwashed hands and his boots smelt strongly of violets. His mother smelt of the leftover orange she had eaten in the carriage before falling asleep. Years later, when Futh worked in the manufacturing of artificial odours, the smell of octyl acetate would make him feel sad.

He knew, sitting there on the rushing train, that his mother was leaving them. He knew that when the train reached their station, the holiday would be over and then she would go. He wanted the train to slow down; he wanted it never to stop. He wanted his mother to keep on sleeping, his father to stay in the bar. But the train sped on and the daylight went and through the windows, in the dark, Futh glimpsed the names of the stations they were hurrying through and he knew that they were almost home. His father returned from the bar, and the noise he made coming into the carriage looking for his seat woke Futh's mother, and the train slowed, and trundled to a stop.

Futh can't for the life of him remember his mother's favourite song, how it goes, and as he walks from the train station to that night's hotel he keeps humming at it, trying to pin it down. In the end, he almost has it.

Arriving at the hotel in wet boots, he finds that it has an indoor porch where other walkers have left their muddy footwear. He does the same, stowing his in a spare corner for the night.

Getting his key, he goes to his room and straight into the bathroom to run a hot bath. While he waits for the tub to fill he looks around the bedroom. He approves of the décor. The curtains and the bedding are made of the same material, with a nature theme which is echoed in the watercolour over the bed and the embroidered cover of the cushion on the armchair. The colours are picked out in the paint on the walls and the woodwork. He appreciates such womanly touches. He would like something like this in his flat.

He is satisfied by the sight of a fire escape immediately outside the window.

He undresses, packing his clothes straight into his suitcase, trying to keep the clean things separate from the dirty things. He thinks about doing some stretches like he used to have to do at school before running. He tries to touch his toes but can't quite reach them and even then it hurts the backs of his legs. At first this makes him feel old, but then he recalls not being able to do it at school either. He was never any good at running anyway. He sits down on the edge of the bed and does some ankle exercises but they are excruciating.

He goes into his suitcase and takes out his alarm clock, sets it for the morning and puts it by the bed. On his way back to the bathroom, he stops by the window to look at the view beyond the fire escape – the night sky, the dark hillside, the moonlit river. He thinks of opening the window to let the night air in and discovers that the window frame is painted shut.

He steps gingerly into the tub, his raw heels stinging. As he lowers himself in, slowly reclining his weary torso, the deep water rises up. It washes against his jaw and his cheeks like waves against the hull of a boat and closes over his head.

CHAPTER TEN

MEMORABILIA

Ester strides along the pavement, the heels of her new stilettos beating like tiny war drums against the concrete slabs.

She began her afternoon at the hairdresser's, where she had her hair cut short again and bleached the platinum blond she had worn in her early twenties. The girl tried to persuade her to have a warmer shade, but Ester was adamant.

Afterwards, browsing the clothes shops, Ester found herself looking at a window display, at a mannequin wearing a strapless dress with a corset bodice and a knee-length skirt, satin in her favourite shade of pink, like the Blushing Pink she had chosen for the bedroom walls. She stood there on the pavement for a while, looking in through the window at the dress and at the mannequin whose hard, expressionless face was turned away from her.

It was some time since she had been shopping for clothes. She took the dress to the changing room, pragmatically choosing one a size larger than she had been the last time she wore anything like this, before buying the dress one size larger than that. She also bought some shoes, the same shade with a stiletto heel.

She stopped at a café for a sandwich and a beer. She went into the toilets to change into her new outfit, noticing that her dress matched the toilet paper. Leaving her old clothes and shoes behind, she set off home.

Marching through Hellhaus in ten-centimetre heels, she knows she does not look like the girl she once was. The hairdresser was right. The severe cut and cold blond now make her look tired. She is broader and heavier than she was and her calves are fleshy beneath the hem of her new dress. But she walks with the same swing in her arms, the same sway in her hips, and her flesh and bones remember something of herself at twenty-one.

She was aware of Bernard before she met him. He was always a topic of conversation at Ida's house. When Ester was not at Ida's, she was often with Conrad and his friends, who also knew Bernard. Someone would ask about him, or someone would have news or gossip about him, about what he was doing, who he was with, when he was coming home. Bernard was only a little older than his brother, but Ester sometimes thought that he made Conrad – who still lived at home with his mother and still knocked about with his schoolmates – seem like a child.

She met a few of Bernard's ex-girlfriends, all of whom were thin and blond and well-dressed. She heard stories about him punching boys for talking too long to his girl-friends, and one about him pushing a stranger down a flight of stairs for just looking. 'He hit me with a bottle,' one boy told her, showing off a faint scar above his eyebrow, 'for dancing with his girl.'

After she and Bernard became a couple, he was jealous around her too. He did not like other men looking at her, although he never hit them, and Ester wondered why not, why he had cared more about his previous girlfriends.

On their first date, they saw a film, and Ester kept the cinema ticket, at first just in her purse and later in an envelope with everything else – a few postcards, a beer mat on which he had written his telephone number, a dried flower from a walk they had taken, and a dead leaf she had found in her hair afterwards.

She still has these things. She keeps them in the drawer of her bedside table and looks through them sometimes, putting the dry flower to her nose. She handles the envelope's contents reverently as if these were the memorabilia of a dead pop star rather than the man she married, the man she still lives with.

Bernard, she thinks, would not recall now which film they saw on their first date, might not even remember that they went to the cinema on that occasion. The young Bernard, lying in a field beside her, turning towards her and holding a cornflower against her cheek, near the blue of her eye, seems almost like a different man, a lover she once had. She keeps him in an envelope in a drawer, that man who admired her calves; that man who, twisting the cornflower between his thumb and his index finger, said, 'Come away with me.'

He used to fall asleep holding on to her, the weight of an arm and a leg pinning her to the mattress, the heat between them almost unbearable. Now he turns away, wants his space. Sometimes he wears a sleep mask and earplugs. These days, Bernard only notices Ester when other men do.

Ester does not normally enter the hotel through the front door, but today she does. She strides across the room, her heels beating time against the wooden floorboards. She walks towards the door at the side of the bar which leads to the bedrooms, and out of the corner of her eye she sees Bernard turning and watching her.

As she walks along the upstairs corridor, she hears the creak of the stairs behind her. She goes through the door marked 'PRIVATE' and into her and Bernard's apartment. She waits in the bedroom.

She hears Bernard letting himself in and moments later he appears in the doorway. 'What's all this for?' he asks, his gaze sweeping over her like a searchlight. He comes closer. 'Who are you trying to impress?' He holds her by the upper arms and squeezes, twisting her flesh a little, as if juicing an orange. Ester says nothing, just looks him in the eye until he relaxes his grip. She turns away so that he can undo the zip in the back of her dress. He does it slowly, and perhaps this is supposed to be seductive but she can only think that he is distracted by something or that he is warily delaying the moment when she will be undressed.

With Ester's zip undone, Bernard walks round to his side of the bed. He closes the curtains but the room remains light. He sits down on the edge of the mattress to unlace his shoes, unbuckle his belt, unbutton his shirt. He looks at Ester and looks away. She steps out of her shoes and slips off her dress and stands by the bed in her knickers.

Bernard pulls back the covers so that she can get under. She can feel where he held her, where his fingers pressed into her skin, where the evidence, the small, round bruises, will be later. The heel of one foot, rubbed by her new shoes, bleeds lightly into the bedsheet.

Bernard, naked now, takes off his watch, stopping to wind it before putting it down on the bedside table. He gets into bed and turns towards Ester. He looks at her as if she reminds him of someone, as if he is trying to remember who. *It's me*, she wants to say to him, *I remind you of me*.

His camphor smell fills her nostrils, and his eyes close.

CHAPTER ELEVEN

DISINFECTANT

Futh takes his breakfast to his table by the window. It is, he notices, brightening up a bit. Settling down, picking up his cutlery, he looks around the room. He sees a woman in her thirties entering, going to the bar. She orders coffee and opens the book she is carrying, reading it where she stands. Futh, working his way through an enormous helping of salami, notices that she has good skin. She is careful, he thinks, in the sun. Angela always wears face cream with built-in UV protection and he wonders if this woman does too. She sips her coffee and Futh glances at the cover of the book she is reading, recognising it as a novel which he has seen in Angela's possession.

Polishing off his salami, Futh stands up and crosses the room, carrying his plate back to the buffet which is laid out at one end of the bar. He would like more. There is a short queue and he joins it, finding himself standing next to the woman at the bar.

'Hello,' he says.

The woman does not respond.

He tries again, asking, 'Enjoying the book?'

She moves her gaze to the top of a new page, turning her head slightly away from him.

Even though the title of this woman's book, like Angela's, is in English, he rephrases the question in German. 'Good book?' he says, and then stands there awkwardly, his plate held out in front of him like a begging bowl. His hand goes to his pocket, seeking out and wrapping itself around the silver lighthouse.

He says, going back to English, 'You wear the same perfume as my wife.'

She looks up, and her gaze drops down to his trousers, to the hand which is deep inside his pocket, gripping the silver lighthouse, his thumb anxiously circling its smooth, warm dome. Futh, noticing that the queue for the buffet has gone, moves on.

Back in his room, Futh sits on his bed and touches the painful parts of his feet. Seeing his sandals in his suitcase, he takes them out and tries them on with a pair of socks. Even without plasters, the sandals are heavenly; they do not rub his wounds.

When he leaves the hotel, he leaves his walking boots behind in the porch, not even glancing back at them. He is not expecting to see any more rain.

He crosses the river again and enters woodland. It is good, he thinks, striding out, to leave things behind. He almost wishes that his suitcase, which is more than half full of dirty washing, was not being sent on to the next hotel. He could manage, he thinks, with what he is wearing and carrying. He could hand-wash his clothes every night in soap in the sink and hang them out of the window to dry.

He could even manage with less than this, he thinks. There are all sorts of things in his rucksack which he could jettison – he does not really need a spare pair of walking socks or a travel sewing kit. He has never used his spork or his compass. He has been carrying a novel around all week and has not even opened it since Hellhaus. He has brought along his swimming trunks and a towel, thinking that he might have a dip in the Rhine, just to be able to say to his father, to Kenny, to his Aunt Frieda, that he did it. But it all looks too deep and fast flowing and far too cold. He does not even think that there is anywhere to paddle.

He has not read his great big guidebook – he never looks to see where he is going. He will read it later, on the ferry home, or he will not read it at all. He once went to Rouen and spent some hours awestruck by the medieval houses, breathing in the history, only discovering later, reading the guidebook on the way back, that the houses were imitations, built after the war.

He is very aware of the silver lighthouse being in his pocket. It has never bothered him before but now he wishes it wasn't there, poking at his groin with every step he takes, its little weight constantly against his leg. It could travel in the suitcase instead, he decides, and then he would be all the lighter.

In his back pocket, he has condoms, 'protection' as his Aunt Frieda used to call them. He does not appear to need any.

He thinks of all the boxes which are no doubt already

waiting for him in his new flat. He wishes they were not there. He would have preferred, at the end of the week, to let himself in and find only the neutrally painted walls, the expanse of stain-resistant carpet and the basic furniture, and not all this stuff which belongs to the past and to a marriage which is over. He wishes he had just left it all behind, let Angela have it or let it be thrown out. In fact, he thinks, he would have preferred not to be going back at all.

As a child, he often fantasised about running away, changing his appearance and his name so that he would not be found, could just disappear. The thought still appeals to him, and he could even do it, he thinks; he could go anywhere, start a new life. He could stay in Germany or go to New York. He could just never go home and Angela and his father and Gloria would wonder what had become of him. He wonders who would be the first to notice his absence.

When his mother left, his father got rid of everything which had belonged to her, anything she had not taken with her. He built a bonfire and lit it before Futh woke up, throwing onto it all her books, photographs still in their frames, the pictures she had never hung, folders full of her Open University work, her pin board with indecipherable lists still attached, even furniture which he smashed first, even clothes and the kitchen curtain material, even her walking boots, and Futh's, adding something to the fire to help it devour these things so that the air stank, filled with searing fumes. He pulled up the flowers and weeds in the bed she had planted and then neglected, in between the climbing frame and the fence. And then, while the bonfire blazed in the garden, he cleaned the house, hoovering and scrubbing until there was nothing left of Futh's mother, only a lingering smell of disinfectant in every room. Although, Futh supposed, there had to be microscopic particles which his father had missed, and there were the books hidden under Futh's mattress – his mother's banned literature – and there was the silver lighthouse which Futh still carried with him everywhere he went.

Looking at his watch, he sees that it is lunchtime. He ate all that salami for breakfast and then, after that awkward exchange with the woman at the bar, he went back to the buffet table and got some more, but when he thinks about it, he could eat again. He wants to eat plenty of meat and carbohydrates, to build up his strength. What he would really like is a big ham sandwich and a homemade cake or pastry, but he only had room in his pockets for a plain roll and a small banana from the buffet. But, he thinks, does he really need any more than that? He could live like this, surely, eating only as much as he really needs to, spending very little, getting by. He sits down in a clearing to eat his lunch and two minutes later it is gone and he feels hungrier than he did when he started. But is it not good, he thinks – a little bit of hunger, fasting – for the soul?

He could live off the land, eating wild meat. People eat squirrel meat, and there is always the river. Or he could be a wandering ascetic surviving on roots and berries. But, thinks Futh, don't some of them die? They starve to death, or go missing in deserts.

He thinks about the big meals Gloria made for just the two of them after his mother left. Despite his father, Futh had begun to go to Gloria's house as often as he could come suppertime. Sometimes she gave him drinks, wanting him to try a new liqueur or a cocktail, and sometimes she fed him. Even if he'd had supper with his father, he still went over to Gloria's for more. 'You're hollow,' she told him, 'you young boys.'

Futh had supposed that Kenny – whose father's work had always meant a lot of travelling and who had sometimes been in Europe for weeks and months at a time – was living a long way away. He had expected postcards and letters with foreign postmarks. He had started collecting stamps although so far he only had one from his Aunt Frieda.

But now Futh was quite often at Gloria's kitchen table, in the middle of his second supper, when Kenny came in, dropped off by his father after football practice or jujitsu or some other activity. Kenny lived, it turned out, just a few miles away and regularly spent a night at his mother's.

Kenny would eat but then he would go to his bedroom and shut the door. Sometimes Futh would go into Kenny's room and hang out with him, and sometimes Gloria would say, 'We'd better leave him be. We'll keep each other company.'

Kenny had started smoking. Futh, going into Kenny's bedroom, found him leaning out of the window so that the smoke would go outside. He went over and stood beside him, looking out at the back of his own house, inside which his father was crashed out on the sofa, the only light – flickering, flashing – coming from the television whose sound Futh had turned down before coming out.

Kenny was making smoke rings, blowing them out of the window, blowing one in Futh's face, and Futh closed his eyes as the smoke enveloped him.

'Here,' said Kenny, passing the cigarette to Futh, who took it.

When Gloria, whose footsteps Futh had not heard on the stairs, opened the door saying, 'Are you smoking in here?' Kenny was on the bed, reading a bike magazine. Futh did try to say that he had not been the one smoking but Gloria was not having any of it. 'You've been caught red-handed,' she said. 'Either you've been smoking in here or you were just about to.'

She sent him home to his father. 'I'm going to call him,' she said, 'and tell him why I've sent you home.' And even though Futh had never so much as put a cigarette to his lips, he knew he was going to be punished for it. It was only much later that Futh wondered why Kenny, hearing Gloria coming up the stairs, had not just dropped the cigarette out of the window.

On one occasion, Gloria rented a video which Kenny wanted to see, and Futh was to see it as well and to sleep over afterwards. Futh's father had not been keen on the idea but Gloria had spoken to him, had taken care of it.

Futh packed his pyjamas, his toothbrush, his sleeping bag and his torch, none of which he would end up using. Gloria made slabs of ham with apple sauce and they all sat together in the kitchen to eat. When they had finished, she sent the boys into the living room to draw the curtains and put in the video while she made popcorn. 'You've got to have popcorn with a film,' she said to Futh, 'haven't you?'

'Yes,' said Futh, even though the smell of popcorn made him feel nauseous.

Kenny took the video out of its box and pushed it into the player and then sat sullenly at one end of the sofa with the remote control. Futh closed the curtains and sat down at the other end, leaving space for Gloria in between them. He wanted to wait for her but Kenny was already playing the video and would not stop it. While the trailers were on, Futh picked up and unscrewed the lid of a pot of Gloria's hand cream which was on the arm of the sofa. He put the pot to his nose to smell its blissful scent of tangerines, all the more potent in the dim room.

'Why are you here?' said Kenny.

Futh, surprised, said, 'You asked me over.'

'No I didn't,' said Kenny. 'My mum invited you.' He looked at Futh who was still holding the hand cream. 'Stop smelling that,' he said. 'Stop touching her things.' Futh put the pot down but Kenny was standing up anyway. 'I'm going to my room,' he said. He left, and Futh reached for the remote control left behind on a cushion, pressing 'pause'.

Gloria appeared in the living room doorway with a bowl of popcorn in her hands. 'Where's Kenny?' she asked.

'I don't think he wants to watch the film,' said Futh.

Gloria went to Kenny's room and when she came back she said, 'Did you two have a fight?'

'No,' said Futh. He had started toying again with the pot of hand cream.

'Well, he's being difficult,' she said. 'You don't want to watch this with just me, do you?' But even as she said this, she was advancing with the popcorn. Futh wondered if he should go and talk to Kenny in his room. Perhaps he should just go home. But Gloria was settling down next to him, unpausing the video. The film was starting and he did not move. She put the bowl of popcorn in her lap, telling Futh to help himself. 'I always make too much,' she said, 'and it's just the two of us now.' She retrieved her pot of hand cream, dabbing some onto the back of each hand and rubbing it in and the smell of popcorn got mixed up with the smell of tangerines.

Futh fell asleep on the sofa, on Gloria, and Gloria must have put him into bed with Kenny rather than into his sleeping bag on the floor because that's where he was when he woke up in the morning and Kenny was pulling back the covers and saying, 'Fucking get out.'

After that, Kenny's visits to Gloria's house never coincided with Futh's. Futh, opening Gloria's back door, would ask if Kenny was around, but Kenny was always at his father's or out doing something. 'But,' said Gloria, 'come in anyway and keep me company.'

Futh, feeling peckish, stops to pick some blackberries, eating them quickly so that he won't think about the grubs which might be inside them. When he reaches into the bush for more, unseen thorns tear his skin, the palm of his hand. Extricating himself, he walks on, sucking at the scratches, without his second helping of blackberries. It is only when he stops to look at his map and sees the red smear he leaves across it, when he looks at his hand and sees the blood still coming out of him, that he realises how deep the wound is. But still, he thinks, as he shrugs off his rucksack and takes out his first-aid kit, opening a packet of disinfectant wipes, this is nothing compared with the way a head wound bleeds.

Not long after the sleepover, he ran into Kenny unexpectedly when, following Angela home from school, Futh missed his turning and ended up on a strange estate. Afterwards, looking at an A to Z, he would be astonished to see how close to home he had been, but at the time he didn't know where he was, could only guess which way to go, and set off in a direction which would take him a long way round, taking the wrong alleyway out of the estate.

The alleyway had six-foot walls on either side, although here and there it was lower where the bricks had fallen away, and it curved so that Futh could not see all the way from one end to the other. He was more than halfway down it when he caught the smell of cigarette smoke, and as he rounded the bend he saw Kenny standing against the wall blowing smoke rings.

At first it looked as though Kenny was on his own, but then Futh, following the alleyway's curve, saw that there were other boys with him, leaning against the wall or sitting on top of it where it was lower. Futh recognised some of them from school, and a part of him wanted to turn around or climb over the wall, to go another way, but he didn't, he just kept moving forward like a train on a track.

He thought that Kenny might ignore him, or even worse make fun of him in front of these boys, tell them about him wetting the bed in his sleep, or perhaps he already had. He wondered whether he should stop and say hello or if he should just put his head down and keep moving.

As he neared the group, he saw Kenny see him, and as he slowed, one of the boys said something which made the others look at Futh and laugh. Futh, drawing level with Kenny, caught the look in his eye and kept walking, stepping over and around the litter and rubble. An empty drink can bounced off his shoulder, followed by a chunk of broken brick striking him on the back of his head.

He arrived home with blood on his fingertips, having touched them to his scalp where it hurt. He went to the bathroom cabinet and took out the disinfectant, soaking a cotton wool ball with it. His mother had done this countless times, cleaning him up while he sat on the edge of the bath. He felt for the wound and pressed the cotton wool ball against it, closing his eyes when the soothing sting came.

His father, perhaps having seen the contents of the bathroom bin or perhaps just noticing the state of the back of his son's head, made Futh tell him what had happened. 'You need to learn how to take care of yourself,' he said.

Futh picked up a few leaflets, considering jujitsu or something like that, but it was not really his thing.

Futh did not see Kenny again until they met at the university open day. And they did not really keep in touch even after that, but Gloria talked about him. Futh learnt that, after school, Kenny got a job at a petrol station, and later at a bicycle repair shop, that he got married, had children, and completed a training course at a local college, becoming a mechanic.

When Kenny was taken on at a second-hand car dealership, Gloria said to Futh, 'When you need a car you should go there. He can get you a discount.' Futh sometimes thought about going and looking at second-hand cars, seeing Kenny, but he couldn't drive and he put it off until he was in his forties, and then when he did buy a second-hand car, he went elsewhere.

Packing away his first-aid kit and going on his way, picking blackberry seeds out of his teeth, Futh thinks about the grubs he has just eaten, and Carl saying, 'Do you ever get a bad feeling about something and then it happens?'

He rather liked Carl. He considers ending his walking tour a day early and going to Utrecht, to Carl's mother's clean, sparse apartment, spending some time with them and sleeping over, giving Carl a lift to the ferry on the Saturday. But he does not know Carl's telephone number or his last name and he has not noted Carl's mother's address. As much as he likes the idea, he puts it aside, expecting instead to see him on the return ferry.

As he walks, the dressing he applied to the palm of his hand catches repeatedly on the zip on the side pocket of his trousers. By the time he reaches that night's stop, the dressing is gone and his wound is bleeding again, onto his trousers.

In his hotel room, he puts more disinfectant on his wound, and a clean dressing. He changes his trousers, taking the silver lighthouse out of his pocket and putting it away in his suitcase.

He opens the window and stands there for a while, taking in the view and watching the people, mostly couples, who are walking and stopping to look at menus and displays in the windows. He is directly above the gently sloping, ivy-covered roof of the hotel's porch. The window is small, perhaps too small to fit through, but there is a larger window further along the same wall. As he heads for the door, he peers through this larger window and sees spike-topped railings underneath.

He wanders downstairs and goes outside, stopping to look at a nearby shop's postcard stand. He chooses a picture of a flower market for Angela, a picture of an apple stall for his father, a view of the Rhine for Aunt Frieda. He buys stamps and a pen. He eats alone at a table for two in a big, windy square and writes his postcards while he drinks his coffee. When he has finished, he puts away his pen, and touches, out of habit, his empty trouser pocket, and then he lifts his hand, with its new dressing, its whiff of disinfectant, to his nose.

CHAPTER TWELVE

ROMANCE

Ester sits on her stool at the bar with a gin and tonic. Her hand keeps straying to her hair, which now seems very short and white and makes her look, she has begun to think, like her father.

She is wearing old clothes and her flats because she can't do the rooms in a nice frock and heels. But after her drink she will go upstairs, take a nap and then change, putting on the pink satin dress and her heels and a little perfume. She has resolved to make an effort every day now. She will do it today even though Bernard is not there to notice. It makes her feel good, and there is always someone who looks, who appreciates her effort.

Bernard is out of town for two nights. He has gone to his mother's and he always goes alone.

Ester goes upstairs, slips off her shoes and lies down on her side of the bed. She picks up the book on her bedside table – a romance. She collects Mills and Boons, has hundreds of them. She finds her place and begins to read. Turning onto her side, facing Bernard's half of the bed, moving closer to his pillow, she breathes deeply, inhaling the faint scent of him. Reaching behind her for the small bottle of camphor oil she has moved from the side of the bath to her bedside table, Ester puts a few drops on the corner of his pillowcase.

This is something she does when Bernard is away from home, keeping the smell of him in her bed. Some people do not like the smell of camphor; for others it is addictive. It is used, amongst other things, as a moth repellent and as an aphrodisiac.

She settles down again, lying with her face on the edge of his pillow, one arm stretched out across the empty bed.

She has tried to write a romance. She has several drafts of a novel in the drawer by her bed, but none of them, she thinks, is any good. She has never shown them to Bernard. Ester does not like her heroine, and her ending is not right. She takes these attempts out of the drawer from time to time and looks at them, changes something or starts a new draft. She did begin a different story but she did not even change the woman's name – it was really just another abortive draft of the same story to put away in her drawer.

She wakes with her face buried in Bernard's pillow, the corner of her Mills and Boon poking into her. She is famished.

She takes off her work clothes and sits down at her dressing table to redo her make-up before putting on her new dress. Then, stepping into her heels, Ester heads down to the bar.

She is expecting a guest – single room, one night, bed

and breakfast – at the end of the afternoon. In the meantime, it is quiet. The new girl is behind the bar. Other than her and Ester, the place is empty except for an elderly couple sitting in the bay window reading guidebooks and leaflets. Ester, parking herself on her stool, asks the girl to fetch her a drink and a couple of bags of peanuts.

Bernard hired her almost a year ago but he still calls her 'the new girl', and Ester does too. The girl is about twenty, slim, long-limbed. She has her hair in a ponytail and wears no make-up. She has lovely skin. Ester watches her, mesmerised by her youth. She wonders if Bernard has ever looked at the girl this way. She has never seen him do so. Ester straightens her back and crosses her legs. She feels heavy. Her make-up feels thick on her skin. She feels overdressed. Looking down at her magnificent shoes, she sees the veins bulging in her feet, the broken capillaries in her calves.

The elderly couple finish their drinks, gather their things and leave. Ester watches them walking past the window holding hands and laughing about something. She drinks her gin and the hands of the huge clock on the wall move silently round.

The guest arrives at five. When he opens the door, the late afternoon sunshine streams in with him. He has come a long way with a heavy rucksack but he is fit and strong. He is young, younger than Ester but not as young as the new girl. As he approaches the bar he takes a piece of paper out of his pocket and offers it to the girl. 'I have a room booked,' he says. He speaks in English and the girl does not understand but she smiles at him.

'It's me you want,' says Ester.

He looks at her doubtfully and then back at the girl, who smiles again and tucks a stray strand of hair behind her ear.

Ester climbs carefully down from her stool and walks over to her guest, her shocking-pink heels banging loudly against the bare floorboards in the quiet room. She stands close to him, and leans closer to read the paper which he still holds out to the girl. She can feel the warmth in his skin, and the hairs on his arm against her own. 'Yes,' she says. 'Come and sit down. Have your meal and then I will show you to your room.'

She takes the boy to a table for two and sits him down, then she goes to the kitchen to fetch his plate of cold meats from the fridge. Returning to the bar, she removes the cling film, slides the plate onto the table in front of the boy and sits down opposite him. 'Go ahead and eat,' she says. When he hesitates, she reaches over, takes a piece of sausage from his plate and holds it up to his mouth, saying, 'Try some of this.' When he does not open his mouth for her, she brings her hand back and puts the morsel in her own mouth. 'It's very good,' she says.

She has the girl bring drinks. When the girl puts them down on the table, Ester sees her glancing at the boy and catches a flicker of a smile before she goes back to the bar. Ester leans forward and picks a strip of ham off the boy's plate. 'Oh, the ham is good,' she says, not offering it this time but putting it directly into the boy's mouth, poking it between his lips. She feels his teeth against her fingertip.

The boy eats then, quickly and silently, before pushing back his chair, his meal only half-finished, saying, 'I'd like to go to my room now.'

'Yes,' says Ester, sucking a greasy fingertip. 'Come with me.' She walks to her desk, puts a tick in her ledger and takes his key down from its hook. 'You're in number ten,' she says, and then adds, 'right next to my room.' She takes the rucksack from between his feet and carries it to the lift. While he insists that there is really no need, she stands inside the lift with his bag, waiting until he joins her. When he does, she presses the button and the doors close.

Now it is just the two of them in the quietly rising lift. 'If there's anything you need,' she says, 'just let me know.'

She carries his rucksack down the corridor to the end room and waits while he fumbles the key into the lock and opens the door. She takes his rucksack inside and puts it down on the bed. Knocking on the wall just above his headboard, she says, 'If you need anything at all.'

'I won't bother you,' he says. He has not yet come into the room. He is standing by the door, holding it open.

'You wouldn't be bothering anyone,' she says. 'My husband's away.'

He nods, and when still she remains with one hand on his rucksack, he says, 'Oh, right,' and puts his hand in his trouser pocket. Finding a note of the lowest denomination, he holds it out.

She moves away from the bed then and comes towards

him. Passing him in the doorway, she says, 'Goodnight,' and leaves him with the money still in his hand.

Back downstairs, she eats the boy's leftovers for her supper. She usually goes to bed before the bar closes. If there are no customers and Bernard is away she sometimes tells the new girl to call it a night and get off home. The place is empty tonight, but when the girl suggests closing early, Ester says no, they should stay open, someone might still come in. She stays perched on her bar stool, watching the girl, who has nothing to do. Not until the big clock says it is closing time does Ester say, 'All right then. Go home.' The girl lifts the stools up onto the tables and fetches her coat and bag, and Ester, on her way to bed now, says to the girl, 'Lock the door on your way out.'

Ester has a quick bubble bath before getting into bed. She drops off quickly before being woken by a gentle tapping sound which builds to frenetic hammering against the partition wall.

CHAPTER THIRTEEN

CIGARETTE SMOKE

It looks as if it is going to be a warm day. Futh is wearing his sandals again but without the socks, and his naked feet glow white between the straps. Even at nine o'clock in the morning the sun is quite strong. He feels it warming the back of his neck above his collar, and the backs of his knees beneath his shorts, as he walks to the outskirts of the town.

Passing a postbox, he drops in the cards he wrote the evening before. He will, he thinks, be seeing his father and Aunt Frieda and Angela before their postcards reach them, but still, this is the sort of thing one does on holiday. He has included Gloria on his father's card but he has not written to Kenny.

Even after Futh's father moved in with Gloria, Futh did not see much of Kenny, who generally avoided their family get-togethers, never attending his mother's soirées or coming for the Sunday dinners Futh's father cooked. But then Kenny, even in his twenties, had his own family, children, and Futh, as it was pointed out, did not.

But when Futh was visiting his father, he always found

an excuse to get out of the house for an hour, and seeing as Gloria lived near Kenny, Futh did see him from time to time.

On one occasion, Futh was in the supermarket buying meat and potatoes and bottles of wine for his father's Sunday lunch. Following the piped fresh bread smell to the bakery section, he came across Kenny selecting bread rolls, squeezing them and then putting them back.

'How are you?' asked Futh.

'Hungry,' said Kenny, picking up an iced bun with his oil-stained hand and replacing it with his thumbprint in the icing. 'You?'

'I'm seeing someone,' said Futh. 'In fact, you've met her. She was at that university open day – the girl I knew from school.'

Kenny investigated a cake, put his finger in the butter-cream and licked it off. 'The girl who didn't remember you,' he said. 'You're seeing her?'

'I bumped into her again,' said Futh.

While Kenny was picking through the gingerbread men, Futh asked after his wife and children and Kenny pointed out a woman in the biscuit aisle with twin boys who looked just like Kenny.

Futh, meanwhile, had put three iced buns in a bag and it was only as he was walking away that he realised he had got the one on which Kenny had left his thumbprint. He felt awkward about going back and swapping it in front of Kenny, so he just carried on to the checkout, knowing that he would have to eat that one.

He saw Kenny again on a nearby industrial estate where

there was a store selling camping and outdoor equipment. Futh liked to browse in this sort of place and think about taking up climbing or kayaking, imagining trekking alone in the mountains or riding the rapids in a one-man canoe. This was before he was married to Angela. He looked at the tents, and sometimes he bought something small – gloves or a torch. He also bought all kinds of guidebooks and manuals. On this particular day, he had, amongst his purchases, a five hundred page hardback on ice climbing and a last-minute addition of a guide to self rescue, some big batteries and a spork. Walking away from the store, he passed a parked car and saw Kenny in the passenger seat. He went closer to the side window to catch Kenny's attention but paused before knocking. There was a woman in the driver's seat, but he couldn't tell whether it was Kenny's wife. She had her hands over her face and was partially obscured by Kenny who had his arm around her. She was upset but Kenny was saying something which seemed to help. The window was open a crack and Futh caught the smell of Kenny's cigarettes. The woman dropped her hands, reaching into her bag for a tissue, and Futh, not wanting to disturb them, continued on his way, walking the mile back to the flat with the handles of his carrier bag cutting into the palms of his hands.

He wonders what Angela is doing at this moment, then he realises that at just after nine on a Thursday morning she will be working. She will not be thinking of him.

Angela, having considered science at the local university, studied English for one term at another institution.

Then she switched again and went back to biology, ending up in publishing, in the editorial office of a scientific journal. It has never really suited her. She has always complained about it. Sometimes she has specific grievances and sometimes she is just generally dissatisfied. She has always kept an eye on the vacancies in the paper, circling some of them, rather randomly, it seems to Futh. He has never really known what she wants.

On the honeymoon, when the hire car broke down, they opened up the bonnet and stood in the pouring rain looking despairingly at the lifeless engine, and Angela said, 'I wanted to go somewhere hot.'

'You should have said so,' said Futh. 'You told me you'd be happy with anything.'

'But not this,' she said.

Futh went to the glove compartment and found Angela's manual and the page which depicted the engine. He went back to the front of the car and stood there for a long time looking mostly at the diagram, peering warily at the engine itself from time to time.

Angela said, 'We need Kenny.'

Futh unscrewed an oily cap. He had a good look at it and at the thing he had taken it off and then screwed it back on again, his hands dirty now.

'We don't need Kenny,' he said.

Angela did not look so sure.

When Futh finally learnt to drive, in the last year of his marriage, he bought a second-hand car through the classified ads in the local paper. Gloria said he ought to have taken

Kenny with him, to check the car over before he bought it. Kenny might have spotted the various faults which the car turned out to have.

The very first time Futh tried to drive it to work he had barely gone a mile before he realised that he had a flat tyre. He wondered whether he had bought a car with a slow puncture. He had never had to change a tyre before but he was determined to do it himself. He took out his spare and the jack and with the help of the manual he managed it. He put the tools and the flat away in the boot of the car, feeling very pleased with himself. He was filthy though. He had oil and grime on his hands, under his fingernails, and on his clothes. He decided to go home and shower and change before going on to work.

He parked in a space near his house. As he turned off the engine, he was surprised to see his front door opening. Angela ought to have left for work soon after him, but she was pregnant again and he wondered if she had felt unwell. He was just about to open the car door and get out when he saw that it was not Angela coming out of the house but Kenny, smoking a cigarette. Kenny seemed to look right at him through the windscreen and Futh felt a reflexive desire to hide. Then Kenny turned away, closing the front door behind him and dropping the stub of his cigarette onto the doorstep, and Futh wondered whether the sun was glaring off the windscreen so that Kenny could not see him after all. Without looking again in Futh's direction, Kenny checked his fly and walked away.

After a minute, Futh got out of his car. Glancing at the still-smouldering fag end on his doorstep, he let himself into his house. He stood unmoving in the smoky hallway for a while and then went upstairs. The bedroom door was wide open. Angela was dressing, and he watched her, looking at her body become strange.

When she noticed him, she jumped and said, 'What are you doing here?' Glancing at the untidy bed, she did not wait for a reply before saying, 'I've only just got up. I wasn't feeling well. It's morning sickness, I suppose.'

The bedroom smelt of cigarette smoke and he said so. 'I wish you wouldn't smoke,' he told her, coming into the room to straighten the covers on the bed.

It was Angela who, not long after this visit of Kenny's and in the run-up to Christmas, said to Futh that she thought they should separate, and Futh was astonished. Later, though, he thought about how often he had caught her rolling her eyes or sighing, and he thought that perhaps, having seen all this before, he should have seen it coming.

His father and Gloria said, 'But what about the baby?' and Futh said that they had lost it, a phrase which did, he supposed, suggest some degree of culpability; perhaps it was like losing a ship which failed to face down some natural or man-made disaster.

It was agreed that Futh would be the one to move out, but he did nothing about it for months on end. It was Angela who finally found him a flat to move into and packed up his belongings and arranged for a removal firm to come and take them away.

He applies some sun cream to his neck and his legs, and

then, with the sense that it is all downhill from here, he shoulders his rucksack again and sets off.

He is not carrying any lunch. He did not pocket anything at breakfast that morning, having eaten in a small, quiet dining room under the gaze of the proprietor. He is not aware of having passed a bakery on his way out of town and does not want to turn back and walk any further than he has to looking for one. The day's hike is a relatively easy one. He expects to be at his next stop by mid-afternoon when, he decides, he will eat a late lunch and enjoy a rest.

He is nearing the end of his circular walk now. Tomorrow he will be back at Hellhaus and then he will be going home. Except that he will not be going home, he will be going to his new flat. He thinks of the big front door shared by all the tenants, and the hallway, the concrete floor onto which the bills and circulars drop. He thinks about the buzzers and pigeonholes with these strangers' names written underneath them on little slips of paper. The name on his, he thinks, will be missing, or somebody else's name will be there instead. He thinks about his unknown predecessor, and the bed whose mattress is stained by and sags from the weight of the strangers who have been there before him. At least the flat is furnished. There are cupboards and drawers into which he will put his belongings which, at present, are wrapped and packed into boxes which Angela has labelled. There are carpets and curtains but no lightshades. There is a sofa but there are no cushions. There is a kettle and a microwave oven but no washing machine. There is a television and a phone line but no phone.

It reminds him of his first student flat, except that he did not live alone there.

He thinks of the things he needs to do. He needs to buy plates and cups and cutlery, although he could make do, at first, with paper plates and plastic cutlery, disposable things. He needs cushions and bedding, lightshades and lightbulbs. Perhaps, he thinks, he ought to have wine glasses and coffee-table books. He needs to get a phone connected, and to write his name on little bits of paper and put them on his buzzer and his pigeonhole.

By midday, the heat is quite fierce. There is not a single cloud in the blue sky. Futh puts sun cream on his already peeling skin – on his face and up beyond the receding line of his thinning hair. His father, who is now almost eighty, still has pretty much a full head of hair. Futh wonders whether he takes after his granddad, the one who never made it home. Ernst said that he did. Futh only remembers his granddad as a balding man close to death.

In the early afternoon, Futh notices that his feet are burnt. The skin is hot and pink between the straps of his sandals, and still blue-white underneath the straps, like the perfect band of pale skin on a ring finger when a wedding ring is removed for the first time in years.

It is also then that he realises that he is lost.

He stands in a field looking at his map, looking around for the features which ought to be there but are not. He has no sense of direction. But he does have that compass, which he now fishes out of a side pocket of his rucksack. He cannot get any sense out of it though and finally realises that it is broken. He looks up at the sun. It is high in the sky and does not help him. He turns, gazing back at the path of trampled grass along which he has come. Considering retracing his steps, he wonders about all the points along the way at which he might have made a mistake, missed a turning, lost in thought.

He decides to press on until he finds someone who knows where he is and which way he needs to go. After walking for well over an hour without seeing anyone at all and without any shelter from the sun, he comes, in the middle of the afternoon, to a small village.

Seeing a man standing smoking outside a house, Futh approaches, holding out his map and asking his whereabouts in German. The man takes the map and studies it, his cigarette burning between his lips, ash spilling into the folds of the map. Behind the man, a kitchen window opens. A woman is busy inside. A baking smell wafts out and mingles with the cigarette smoke.

When the man puts his finger on the map, Futh sees just how far astray he has gone. He has been walking in the wrong direction for hours. He has as far to go now as he had when he set out after breakfast – perhaps further, despite walking all morning and half the afternoon.

The man asks him where he has come from and where he is going. Futh tells him and the man says, 'No, you want to be going in the other direction.'

The woman in the kitchen has moved out of sight, and the man is holding out the map for Futh to take back, the cigarette between his fingers burnt down to the filter. Futh, taking the map and thanking the man, walks slowly away, and the smell of cigarette smoke and baking fades until it is gone, leaving only the spilt ash on his fingertips and saliva in his mouth.

His mother smoked on occasion, generally when she finished something big, something difficult. His father did not like the habit and so she smoked furtively. Futh knew of only a handful of instances when she smoked in his whole childhood – when she passed her driving test, when she got her Open University degree, when she finished painting the old house from top to bottom ready for selling. The only time he saw her smoking openly was when they were up on the cliffs in Cornwall just before she left, when she alternated between sunbathing on her back and propping herself up on one elbow with a cigarette.

His father, sitting not far away on a picnic blanket, must have noticed but had not commented on it. Instead, he sat facing the twinkling sea, delivering a monologue on the subject of the lighthouse in front of them.

He talked about lighthouse technology – sunlight and lamplight and the use of mirrors. And he talked about lighthouse keepers, using words and phrases such as 'tending' and 'caring for', so that the lighthouse, in which the lighthouse keeper endlessly polished the many lenses and windows, seemed to Futh a calm place, a safe place, as if the light were one of welcome, a light to guide you home. 'Of course,' said his father, 'it's all automated now,' and it was clear from his tone that he found the automated lighthouse a disappointing substitute for a lighthouse keeper.

He talked about ships which had been wrecked and plundered, some of them not so long ago and perhaps even to this day, despite the lighthouse and its recurrent warnings.

It was scorching. There was a breeze, but when it dropped, the heat was astonishing. Futh, wearing long trousers and walking boots with thick socks, was far too hot. His mother's boots and socks and top were in a heap nearby. His mother was lying on the dry grass with the sun on her bared skin, a tube of sunblock and a packet of cigarettes and a lighter in between her feet. Her eyes were closed so it was hard to tell whether she was sleeping or silently listening to the lecture. But now she opened her eyes and sat up, reaching for her cigarettes. She looked at her husband and made a little noise of exasperation, but he did not notice.

'Every lighthouse,' he said, 'has its own distinctive flash pattern.' Futh wondered whether anyone was expected to remember them all or if there was a manual. You just had to know what you were doing, he supposed, if you were going to go to sea.

His mother rolled her eyes and picked up her lighter, looking at Futh's father, at his profile, as she lit a cigarette, the smell of smoke overwhelming the scent of her sun cream. His father stiffened, paused, and then went on.

'In fog,' he said, 'the foghorn is used.'

Futh, deciding to take a walk, stood up and ambled away. He felt his mother watching him go, but when he glanced back she was not looking at him. He wandered further, until he could no longer hear the drone of his father's voice. He was holding the perfume case which he had taken out of his mother's handbag, the silver lighthouse which his granddad had given to his father. His mother called it 'Uncle Ernst's perfume' as if she were just keeping it safe for him, but she wore it a lot of the time. Futh took the glass vial out of its case. He wanted to smell his mother's scent but he did not remove the stopper.

Futh used to sit in his mother's wardrobe, the floor of which was covered with shoes which seemed never to have been worn, and at one end he made a nest. He closed the doors and sat there with the hemlines of her woollen skirts brushing his face. This, the dark interior of her wardrobe, the smell of leather and secret cigarette smoke and camphor from the mothballs she used in the summer, is what he would have liked to bottle and label 'Essence of Mother', but instead he has violets and oranges.

He was in the wardrobe when he heard his parents coming into their room. He heard their argument through the wardrobe doors. Futh sat very still, safe in this darkness which smelt of his mother, muffled by the woollens. After a while, hearing nothing in the bedroom, he opened the wardrobe door, very slowly and just a little. He saw his mother standing at the end of the bed, looking into her suitcase which was open on top of the bedspread. She stood there for a long time before zipping it up. When she lifted it onto the floor and put it away under the bed, he could tell that it was heavy. He watched her leave the room, heard her go downstairs, and then he climbed out of the wardrobe and pulled her suitcase out again. It was brightly coloured, garish, and he instantly hated it. It was packed with clothes and shoes and toiletries, everything she might need if she were going away. He could tell that she had not just packed it by the creases in clothes which ought to have been hanging in the wardrobe. This was a suitcase which was kept ready-packed as if she might need to make a quick getaway.

Up on the cliffs, there was nowhere to go. The landscape was unbroken. There was no shelter, no shade. He went back, strolling slowly over the grass, holding the silver lighthouse in one hand and the stoppered vial in the other. His father was still sitting looking outwards, facing the lighthouse and the mass of rocks on which it stood. He had fallen silent. His mother had finished her cigarette and was lying on her back again. She looked relaxed. Her face was turned to the sun.

And then his father took a deep breath and began again. 'The foghorn,' he said, 'blasts every thirty seconds.'

'Do you know,' Futh heard his mother say, 'how much you bore me?'

After a moment, in which nothing was said and no one moved, his father stood and began to pack up the picnic, closing the lid on the cool-box, pouring cold dregs of coffee into the grass before putting the lid and the cups back on the Thermos, tossing the empty Pomagne bottle and the uneaten bread and pastry crusts and crumbs over the side of the cliff where they dropped onto ledges and rocks and into the sea and gulls appeared from nowhere, making an incredible noise. He picked up the picnic blanket, shook it out and folded it up.

His wife was still lying in the sunshine with her eyes closed. He walked slowly towards her until he stood above her. His shadow did not touch her and she did not open her eyes. Futh watched the circling gulls swooping down and attacking the scraps, making their din. When he looked, his mother was getting to her feet. She was turned away from him, holding her hand against the side of her face. She said, 'I'm going home.'

She picked up the cool-box and Futh noticed the redness like sunburn on her cheek. Futh's father took the bag and the blanket and walked with her towards the path. Futh looked down and saw the deep cut on the palm of his hand. The glass vial was broken, the perfume stinging in his wound, spilt on the grass and on his hiking boots.

Walking back to the caravan site, lagging behind his parents, he heard them talking although he did not catch much of what they were saying. He heard his father say, 'What about him?' and he saw his mother shrug.

Before the end of the afternoon, they were on the train. His mother, wanting something, looked in the rucksack and found a couple of oranges. She offered one to Futh, who took it, not really wanting it but not wanting to refuse it. He ate it slowly and was still eating it when his mother, having thrown away her peel and wiped her hands, leaned her head against the window and closed her eyes.

That night, back in his own bed, Futh heard his mother in the shower. When she came to his room, standing by his pillow in her dressing gown, her face hanging over him like the moon in the night sky, she no longer smelt of violets or sun cream or the oranges they had eaten on the way home. She smelt of the cigarettes she liked to smoke when she finished something.

When Angela came to bed smelling of cigarette smoke,

it was his mother he thought of, although he knew better now than to say so to Angela. And Angela, he supposed, was thinking of Kenny, whose cigarettes it was she smelt and tasted of.

He retraces his steps, but this time he takes the path which will deliver him to his last stop before Hellhaus. There is no signpost, just an opening in a hedge, a narrow gap leading from one small path to another. He is not surprised he missed it the first time and he is not certain even now that he is going the right way. He begins to feel little but the sting of his sandal straps sawing against his sunburn and his new blisters.

When he finally reaches his hotel he is exhausted. He runs a bath, takes a couple of miniatures out of the fridge in his room and goes onto the balcony. He has a view of the river. He is almost close enough to the water, he thinks, to jump in from here.

He is starving. He has not eaten since breakfast. He looks at the menu from the hotel restaurant and realises that he has just missed dinner. He will have to make do with a bar snack after his bath.

He undresses, selects another bottle from the mini-bar, goes into the bathroom and climbs into the tub. The water is painfully hot and he lies back with a groan and closes his eyes.

He feels as if he is missing something and tries to think what it might be. He missed his father's roast on Sunday. He misses his stick insects, the smell of their vivarium.

Angela will be keeping the stick insects because Futh is not allowed pets at the flat. Angela has never liked the stick insects. She says that they are the kind of thing a school-boy keeps. She finds them creepy, and Futh is worried that she will not look after them properly, that she will forget to feed them.

He wakes feeling chilly. He does not know, for a moment, where he is. Even when he remembers, he is still bewildered because he is lying in an empty tub – all the water must have seeped out around an ill-fitting plug. He has no idea what time it is – his watch is in the bedroom and there is no window in the bathroom, no darkened sky to give him a clue.

His legs have seized up, and he is hungrier than he has ever been – his stomach is growling. His Aunt Frieda used to say, when Futh skipped meals, 'Your stomach will think your throat has been slit.'

He can barely manage to get himself out of the bath, but he does. Hobbling into the bedroom, he sees, through the wide-open balcony doors, the night sky, the moon. He goes outside again for a moment, clinging to the railings and watching the river go by. Listing slightly from the spirits, his stomach complaining, he feels as if he is on a ferry and thinks that he would be very happy never to be on one again.

He can't face calling down for food now. He is too tired to wait for it, too tired to eat. It is not really a bar snack he wanted anyway. He closes the balcony doors and the curtains. As he crawls into bed, he looks at the time and realises that it is already Friday. In twenty-four hours his holiday will be over.

CHAPTER FOURTEEN

VENUS FLYTRAPS

Ester, stirring, smells camphor. Without opening her eyes, she moves closer to Bernard's side of the bed and puts her head on the edge of his pillow, inhaling his scent.

Bernard will not be back until tomorrow. Sometimes he calls at the last moment to tell Ester that his mother needs him, that he will be staying longer.

He visits his mother once a month. When Ester and Bernard were first married, Ester used to go with him, although she found the trips stressful. She was glad to have been invited back into Ida's home but she was unable to think of her mother-in-law without feeling the scrape of the hair pin against her scalp. She used to take a little bottle of gin in her handbag and drink from it when they stopped for petrol and whenever she went to the bathroom.

The very first time they went as a married couple, Ida greeted them brightly at the door. She complimented the flowers Ester had brought for her, displaying them in her best vase on the living room table. She went to make coffee, refusing Ester's offer of help. She said, 'You stay right where you are.' In the morning, Ida brought breakfast in bed. She gave Ester a magazine to read while lunch was being prepared. She would not even let Ester wash up.

Conrad still lived at home and Ester had always hoped to see him during these visits. But each time they went, he made himself scarce. Once, in the car on the way to Ida's, she asked Bernard whether he was expecting his brother to be there. At first he did not respond and much of the journey passed in silence, her unanswered question sinking like cold air in the overheated car. She began to wonder whether she had asked the question out loud. And then, as they neared his mother's house, he said to her, 'Why do you care whether he's there or not? You're with me now. Or have you changed your mind again?'

'Of course not,' she said. But the truth was, she did sometimes wonder whether she had made a mistake. Anyway, she did not see Conrad at Ida's, and she did not ask Bernard about him again, and Bernard never mentioned him.

Over coffee, Ida asked, 'So when can I expect grandchildren?'

Ester, who did not especially want children and thought that she had even said as much to Ida, said, 'Well, we might not have children.'

'But Bernard wants children,' said Ida. She turned to him. 'You'll never guess who I saw last week – Andrea, and she has a little baby boy, he's just beautiful.'

And later, Ida said, 'Bernard, I saw Susanne in the supermarket the other day. She asked after you.' When Ida mentioned these other girls, Ester wondered if one of them was the girl Ida had told her about in the register office toilets, the girl Bernard had loved.

At night, she lay with Bernard on the pull-out bed in the living room, with her head on his rising and falling chest, and she said, 'The day we got married, your mother told me there was only one girl you had ever loved.'

'Well,' he said, 'that's probably true.'

Ester lifted her head to look at him.

'Until you, of course,' he added.

'She said you were only with me to get revenge on Conrad for taking her.'

'Well, maybe that was partly true too, at first.'

Ester lay quietly for a long time, and when she finally said, 'Who was she?' Bernard was asleep, or pretending to be. When Ester broached the subject again in the morning, Bernard became annoyed and would not talk.

At breakfast, Ida said, 'Bernard, Therese has three children now, the girl and twin boys,' and Ester studied his face.

Ida said to Ester, 'You'll lose your figure anyway, if that's what you're worried about.'

On Ester's last visit with Bernard, Ida invited a girl for dinner. The girl came out of the kitchen with two plates of liver, putting one down in front of Ester and giving the other to Bernard. Ida, following her out with more food, said, 'This is Liese. She is a nursery nurse, very fond of children. She is twenty, still young. Although when I was twenty I was already pregnant with Bernard.'

Ester and Bernard always argued on the drive back to Hellhaus.

Eventually, Ester suggested to Bernard that he go to his mother's alone. She made some excuse the first couple of times, but after that she didn't give a reason and he didn't ask for one.

With or without Ester, Bernard always comes home in a bad mood, along with a pile of ironed underpants and paired socks. Ester imagines Ida saying to Bernard what a shame it is that Ester is too busy to come, and couldn't a cheap cleaner have been hired for a couple of days to do what Ester does?

Ester finally opens her eyes and looks at her watch. She gets up and puts on some make-up and the same cleaning clothes she wore yesterday and goes into the bathroom. She runs the tap and fills the saucers of the Venus flytraps which stand on the ledge behind the sink. She brought just one with her from home – one of her mother's plants – dividing and repotting until she had half a dozen. She waters them, and feeds them the dead insects she finds on the windowsills, tickling the leaves to make them close. She drops in flies which she has swatted. Not quite dead, they buzz furiously inside the tightly shut traps, and after a while there is silence. She puts her plants in the sunshine and talks to them, but still they sometimes die.

Opening a window, Ester smokes a cigarette and chats to her plants, her ash falling onto the expectant leaves. The sun is strong even at this hour. It is going to be a hot day.

After breakfasting alone and then checking out the honeymooners who have been there all week and have barely been out except to eat, she cleans their downstairs room. When she has finished, she wheels her cleaning trolley into the lift and goes back to the bar.

She sits on her stool and looks around. There are a couple of customers in. One is a stranger; the other is not. Without taking off her rubber gloves, she has her first gin of the day without tonic. She is hot; she is flushed and damp. She adds tonic to her next one, rolling the icy glass across her forehead and holding it against her breastbone, the condensation trickling into her cleavage.

The door behind her, the door to the guest rooms, swings open. She glances around and sees the boy she put in room ten walking through. He has his rucksack on his back, and his arm around the new girl. Ester goes over to her desk and checks him out, crossing him off in her ledger and returning his key to its hook on the wall. The girl stands at a distance, waiting for him. He seems to be making an effort not to look at Ester, glancing instead at the tired remains of the breakfast buffet beside them, at the sweating meat, the dried-out eggs. Then he and the new girl walk out into the street and the boy puts his arm around the girl's shoulders and Ester watches them walking away.

She drains her glass and removes her rubber gloves.

'Same again?' asks the question mark, moving along the bar towards her. His breath smells of strong coffee. She looks at him, and at the clock, and nods. She leads the way to the lift and they travel up with the cleaning trolley.

She does not take him to her room, will not have him lying on Bernard's side of the bed, lying naked where Bernard sleeps, with his head on the camphor-scented pillow. In room ten, the question mark lies down on the bed, on barely cooled sheets. He undoes his belt and pushes down his trousers, using his feet to get them as far as his ankles. He pulls one foot free but the other one gets stuck and his trouser leg trails from his pale pink shin and Ester thinks of sausage meat and sausage skin. He leaves on his T-shirt and his socks.

Ester, on the other side of the bed, undresses slowly in the bright room while he watches her. When the pieces of her clothing lie around her like the dropped petals of a half-dead rose, she climbs onto the bed.

By the time Ester returns to the bar, the girl is there, serving customers. Ester sits down on her stool and the girl says, 'Bernard's looking for you.'

'Bernard's not back until tomorrow,' says Ester.

'No,' says the girl, 'he's back.'

Ester climbs carefully down from her stool. 'Where is he now?' she asks.

'Upstairs,' says the girl, 'I think.' She turns back to her customer and takes his money.

Ester walks to the lift. Her cleaning cart is still in there. She goes first to their private apartment and finds Bernard's holdall on the end of the bed. She looks in the bathroom, the kitchenette and the little sitting room, but Bernard is not there.

She goes back downstairs and into the bar, picking up her rubber gloves. She goes into the kitchen where the chef is pounding cheap cuts of beef, tenderising steaks for dinner, pulping apples, and smashing black walnuts with a rolling pin, beating them beneath a tea towel to keep the shells from flying, to prevent the juice from staining the work surface.

Ester goes up in the lift again with her cleaning trolley and her rubber gloves. She collects fresh bedding and returns to room ten, cursing quietly to herself. Opening the door, she sees Bernard, who is already walking away from the mess on the bed, the mess he has made of this man who did not leave in time. Passing her in the doorway, Bernard pauses, and she feels the heat of him through his shirt and his breath against her cheek as he leans close to say, 'Don't let there be a next time.'

CHAPTER FIFTEEN

COFFEE

Futh wakes at dawn and can't get back to sleep. He is painfully hungry but knows that the hotel is not yet serving breakfast. He gets up and goes to the table where the coffee-making facilities are and eats the biscuits. Then he makes a cup of instant coffee – coffee whose volatile aromatics have been lost and then replaced during the manufacturing process; coffee to which the smell of coffee has been added – and goes out onto the balcony in his pyjamas to drink it, watching the sun rise, its reflection in the river.

He feels dreadfully stiff and his feet are tender. He thinks seriously about skipping the final day of walking and instead going to Utrecht after all. It would mean arriving unannounced but, he thinks, he was invited. It should not be too difficult to remember the way to Carl's mother's house even without the address, but first he would have to pick up his car which is in Hellhaus. He wonders if he could get a bus to Hellhaus and then drive to Utrecht. He could take his suitcase with him on the bus rather than have it taken by transit and risk it arriving later than him and having to wait for it. If he did that he would not need to go to the hotel at all. He could telephone later from Carl's mother's house and explain his change of plan. If he left here straight after breakfast he might be in Utrecht by lunchtime. Carl, he recalls, would be home in the evening.

He drinks another cup of coffee on the balcony and then gets dressed and goes downstairs, hoping to find the proprietor to ask him for a bus timetable. There is no one about. He finds leaflets promoting places to visit, and a telephone directory in which he looks up his own name, finding other Fuths. But there are no bus timetables. The front door is open though and he wanders outside to look for a bus stop.

He walks slowly and has to go further than he intended, but he eventually finds what appears to be the right stop about a mile from the centre, near the river. He deciphers the timetable and discovers that there are three direct buses to Hellhaus each weekday – one in the morning, one in the early afternoon and one in the evening. He could catch the first one after breakfast.

Feeling pleased, he returns to his room and makes himself one more cup of coffee to see him through. He packs his suitcase, zips it up and puts it by the door. He will collect it after breakfast. With a little bit of time still on his hands, he makes the bed even though he knows it will only be unmade, stripped, when he is gone. Taking one last look around the room, he spots his watch on the bedside table and straps it onto his wrist. He is ready to go.

He heads downstairs, taking his rucksack with him.

While he fills a plate from the breakfast buffet, he stashes in the pockets of his rucksack a few snacks for the bus ride.

He sits down. He is trembling slightly, perhaps from drinking so much caffeine on an empty stomach, but when the hostess offers to bring him a pot of coffee, he accepts. It is good, strong, fresh coffee and the smell brings to mind his mother's grinder, the coffee beans poured into the top and crushed with a turn of the handle.

She always used nice china cups and hot milk poured from a little pan. She used to drink her coffee standing up, looking out of the window. Sometimes an aeroplane would fly overhead and she would watch it, following it across the otherwise empty sky, gazing after it even when it was too small to see and all that remained were the slowly vanishing contrails, lost in a world of her own, as if she were already gone, her coffee cup cold in her hand.

That was how it was when he came downstairs the morning after their return from Cornwall. The kitchen smelt of coffee and she was standing at the window. She was wearing a pink, summery dress which, after looking at her for a while, he recognised from his parents' honeymoon photos – it was her going-away dress. By the back door he saw the garish suitcase from under the bed. His father was still upstairs. And then everything happened in a rush – her kissing him and taking her suitcase and leaving. It happened so quickly that when he picked up her coffee cup in the suddenly empty kitchen, he found that it was still warm.

Leaving the breakfast room, he finds himself shaking

so badly that he needs to sit down. He cannot even contemplate climbing the stairs to his room. Being right by the lounge, he goes in. There is a television in the corner showing the news with no sound, and there are two sofas, neither of them occupied. He lies down on one and closes his eyes and, despite all the caffeine, drifts into a weird sleep.

He wakes feeling anxious. He looks at his watch and is disappointed to see that he has missed the first bus to Hellhaus. He will have to catch the second one after lunch. He will not be in Utrecht, then, before the end of the afternoon, but, he thinks, he is sure to be there in time for his dinner. He rouses himself and goes upstairs to his room.

When he sees that his suitcase has gone, he realises that it must have been taken for transit while he was asleep. He goes back downstairs and asks the proprietor about it and is assured that his suitcase is already on its way to Hellhaus. Well, thinks Futh, if it is already on its way perhaps it will arrive before him. So he will, after all, have to go to the hotel to ask for it and explain what he is doing but that is all right. He might not even have bothered if it had not been for the fact that the silver lighthouse is in it.

He leaves the hotel with some time to kill before catching the afternoon bus. He goes into a shop, thinking of buying a newspaper. He has not looked at one all week and is feeling somewhat detached from reality. The shop has only German papers and Futh, testing his understanding of written German, which is better than his understanding of spoken German, looks through a few but, not making much sense of them, leaves without buying one.

He walks down to the river and sits alone under some trees, appreciating the cool breeze coming off the rushing water. Closing his eyes, he consciously notes the smells around him, the smell of the outdoors, so that he will be able to return later, in his mind, to this oasis.

He has often wondered what it would be like to have an impaired sense of smell. He loves to wake to the smell of fresh coffee, but when Angela was pregnant she became suddenly unable to bear the stink, she said, of the coffee machine, and of Futh unwashed first thing in the morning, for the brief duration of each of her pregnancies. He thinks about things he would prefer not to be able to smell, like alcohol on other people, and he thinks about the potential dangers of being unable to detect certain things, like gas or bad food. Some people cannot smell cyanide. Some people can simply not recognise smells, smelling one thing and interpreting it as something else entirely. It is possible to imagine a smell. He himself, recently, suffering from the flu, found himself smelling coffee which was not there.

He takes out his snacks and eats them for lunch. Seeing some ducks, he breaks up a bread roll and throws the pieces into the water, but the ducks don't notice and the bits of bread are carried away by the current.

When he stands up and leaves his quiet spot between the trees, there is plenty of time to get to the bus stop. His ruined feet go slowly but still he arrives in time and sits down, expecting to see the bus soon.

The minutes go by and he assumes at first that the bus is running late. Then he wonders whether he is standing at the wrong stop, and wanders to the stops either side to have a look at their timetables. Thinking that he might have read the time wrong, or got the wrong day, he looks again at the first timetable, but if he has made a mistake he does not see it. After almost an hour, he decides that either the bus just is not coming or that he arrived a fraction too late – perhaps his watch is a little slow – and the bus had already been and gone by the time he got to the stop.

There is a third and final bus leaving in the evening. He considers whether it will still be possible to go to Utrecht. His hosts, who would not be expecting him, would have had their dinner by the time he got there, although he should not be too late for some supper. He thinks about hitchhiking. He goes to the kerb and stands there for a while with his thumb out, but no one stops. He has not seen a taxi either, and Futh does not really want to walk all the way back into town to try to find one, and besides, it would be expensive, an extravagance for which he has not budgeted. The next bus will be along in a few hours and he decides to wait.

He waits near the bus stop, wishing that he had bought a newspaper after all or that he had not taken the novel out of his bag. He finds some shade, although it moves. He strays into the full heat of the day only when he feels the need to go back to the bus stop and check the timetable again. He catches the evening bus and sits near the back feeling pleased, watching the world go by.

Getting off at what turns out to be the wrong stop, he has a little walking to do before he finally gets into Hellhaus. He sights the hotel from behind as the sun is going down, the sunset blazing on its whitewashed wall, glaring from the windows. It is dazzling, almost painful to look at, but he cannot take his eyes off it.

Before going to the hotel to ask about his suitcase, he goes to check his car. He finds it just where he left it, but it has a flat tyre. Crouching down to investigate, he sees the broken glass in the gutter. Perhaps, he thinks, the glass was already there when he arrived and he parked without noticing it. But, feeling practical now, knowing that he can change a tyre, he opens his boot. Expecting to see his spare, he is dismayed to find instead an old, flat tyre, the same one he removed by the side of the road before driving home to find Kenny coming out of his house.

With a sigh, he gives up his plan to go to Utrecht. He will have to sort his car out in the morning. He walks on towards the hotel to spend the night as per his itinerary, eager anyway for a quiet bar with padded seats and chilled drinks; a bedroom door and a key, a soft carpet and a clean bed and pillows and blankets; a deep bath and a little kettle, a plate of cold sausages and a packet of complimentary biscuits; his suitcase, his silver lighthouse, his pyjamas and rest.

CHAPTER SIXTEEN

MOTHS

Bernard, lying on his side in the grass, touching a cornflower to Ester's cheekbone and comparing its blue to the blue of her eye, said, 'Come away with me.'

She waited only a moment before saying, 'All right,' and, as Bernard touched the cornflower to the blue of her necklace and the blue of the buttons on her blouse, she lay back in the fallen leaves.

She introduced him to her parents. Afterwards, her mother said to her, 'Are you sure, Ester?' and her father said, 'You can still change your mind.'

But Ester did not change her mind. She went with Bernard to Hellhaus. While he ran the pub, she managed the accommodation, taking bookings, receiving guests, doing the housekeeping. There is a cleaner who comes very early each morning and does the bar, the public areas, before breakfast, but Ester takes care of the guest rooms herself.

There is not, in any case, a great deal to do. Of their ten bedrooms, they only ever have a few booked out at any one time. Sometimes rooms stand empty for entire seasons. She once left the light on and the window open in one of the bathrooms and did not go back for weeks. Eventually returning, she found the lightshade – a white glass bowl – full of moths.

When she was a girl, Ester was taken on a visit to the Museum für Naturkunde in Berlin. She was disturbed and fascinated by the museum's extensive collections which included fish and invertebrates preserved in alcohol, stuffed mammals, and butterflies and moths pinned to display boards. A few days later, she was in her room at bedtime with the light still on, reading some romantic photo story in a magazine, when a moth flew in through the open window and began flittering around the light-bulb. This moth, which she pinned to the cork board in her bedroom, was the first in her collection, and the moth collection was the first of her various collections, although what she calls collecting, Bernard calls hoarding.

He is appalled by her bookshelves. He asks her, 'Who needs so many Mills and Boons?'

'I do,' she says.

'Why do you keep all these old lipsticks and perfume bottles?' he says, opening her drawers, doing one of his spot checks. She has never known what he is looking for. Tipping out the contents of the envelope that she keeps in the drawer by her bed, the brittle remains of a dried-out flower falling to the floor, he says, 'What's all this crap?'

Not long after the day she spent lying in the grass with Bernard, Ester arrived in Hellhaus and sought out a doctor. She made an appointment, which was followed by another appointment at a clinic. And while she sat in the waiting room, she thought about those stilled creatures she had seen housed in the museum, an enormous number, and she thought about her own very small collection of night-flying moths. She still recalled the way that first one felt, the tickle of the powdery wings trapped between the palms of her hands.

A few years later, her father suffered a heart attack and died. When Ester went home, her mother said he'd been having palpitations. 'Warning signs,' she said, 'which he ignored.' And, she said, he'd already had one heart attack which had gone unnoticed.

'He didn't notice?' said Ester. 'How could he not notice?'

'Sometimes you don't,' said her mother. 'But the doctor said he'd had one. She could see the damage in his heart.'

At his funeral, Ester's mother, cradling a relative's baby boy in her arms, said to Ester for the first time, 'Where's my grandson?' Since then, she has asked the same question, one way or another, each time she has seen Ester, until recently when she stopped talking about the grandchildren she did not have and instead began giving advice on preserving one's looks in middle age.

Ester does not remember when she started drinking in the morning or sleeping in the middle of the day. She remembers her first infidelity, but she does not remember them all.

She wakes from her nap and sits for some time working on her face in her dressing table mirror, aware that her make-up fails to disguise the dark circles under her eyes and that it probably only draws attention to her crow's-feet and the little lines around her mouth. Is she too old, she wonders, to have children?

She takes out the little wooden lighthouse which Bernard gave to her the morning after their wedding. She had asked Bernard for this vintage perfume, Dralle's Illusion in a lighthouse case, a collector's item, advertised in its day as 'the most costly perfume sold in America'. There were two versions of the lighthouse case – a silver one and a smaller, cheaper wooden one. She was disappointed, on exchanging gifts, to find herself receiving the wooden version.

She applies the violet perfume, beneath which she still smells of the disinfectant with which she cleaned the guest bathrooms. Stoppering the vial, she picks up the silver lighthouse which is now standing beside the wooden one on her dressing table and which is missing its bottle. Putting her vial into the silver lighthouse, she returns the now empty wooden case to the drawer.

She hopes that Mr Futh will not notice his missing item, but if he does and if he mentions it she will tell him that she will talk to the people who transported the luggage. He will have to leave before there is any answer – in the morning, he will be gone.

She puts on her new dress which is beginning to look a little tired. She puts on her heels and some flashy earrings. Bernard does notice, she thinks, although he is barely speaking to her today.

She goes down to the bar and sits on her stool, waiting for Mr Futh, her only guest today. She is expecting him in the middle of the afternoon. She took receipt of his suitcase this morning and has put it at the end of his bed.

As she sips a drink, she notices Bernard looking her way, glancing repeatedly at her legs. Feeling flattered, she subtly adjusts her position so that her legs are well displayed, crossed towards him at the knee. After a while, just as her calves are going numb, the blood, she imagines, pooling in her veins, he heads in her direction and she turns towards him. Bernard, on his way into the back of the hotel, pauses beside her to suggest that she put on some hosiery.

Her mother came to visit once and Ester took her out for a stroll. They walked as far as the ferry point and then went for coffee and cake in the café near the train station. Ester told all the funny stories she could think of and her mother said, 'Come home.'

When it is approaching sundown and Mr Futh has still not arrived, Ester remembers that he was late the previous weekend, although she cannot really remember him, cannot picture him at all.

She has a cup of good coffee in front of her, and an orange. The new girl is behind the bar with not enough to do. Bernard is sitting at a table with a drink and his newspaper, doing the crossword. Ester peels her orange onto the bar and a sweet, citrussy mist surrounds her, masking a warm meat smell. When the door opens, the three of them look up.

A thin man enters. He has caught the sun on his face, even though it is greasy with sun cream. Beneath what there is of his hair, his scalp is bright pink. His feet are in a dreadful state. Ester watches the man hobbling towards the bar. He makes a beeline for the new girl before glancing at Ester and turning in her direction instead.

Even though she has been expecting him, it is not until he is standing in front of her saying hello, saying her name, that she realises that this is Mr Futh. She can feel the heat coming off his skin. He asks for his room and she gives him the key. He says, 'I'd be very grateful if you would bring my supper to my room,' and then, after gazing at his feet for a while as if he is trying to think of something, he walks towards the lift.

She will fetch his supper when she has finished her orange. She turns back to the bar, and the new girl goes back to inspecting her nails, and only Bernard continues to stare at the doorway through which Mr Futh has disappeared.

CHAPTER SEVENTEEN

CAMPHOR

Futh stands in the lift. The door is closed but he has not yet pressed the button which will take him up to his room. He stood in front of Ester feeling very peculiar, no doubt due to sunburn, sunstroke. He thought for a moment that he might be having a panic attack right there in the bar. Remembering his relaxation technique, he looked down at the floor, at his feet, seeing hers, bare on the unswept floorboards, her high heels slipped off. He was unable to concentrate, to focus on his feet, on relaxing his toes and so on. He was disconcerted by her. He stood there too long, staring at her feet, becoming suddenly aware of doing so and limping quickly away to the lift.

Now he stands there, procrastinating, looking at the buttons but not pressing them. He wants to go back and talk to her, about his supper – he wonders whether he ought to tell her that he does not care much for salad. He does not want any to be wasted on his account. Perhaps he should ask her for some after-sun lotion – he would like her to come to his room with a pot of cold cream and, without being asked, dab it onto his sunburn, her cool fingertips soothing his forehead and the back of his neck.

He reaches for the button which will open the lift doors again, before pressing instead the one which will take him upstairs.

In his room, he goes straight over to the bed and sits down. He thinks about lying back but knows that if he does he will fall asleep and wake up there in the small hours or in the morning, still on top of the covers in his shorts and sandals, still in the same position, cold and stiff.

With a great deal of effort, he stands up. Reaching out to open his suitcase, he notices that the zip is not quite done up. He wonders whether he was careless that morning or whether it came undone, or was undone, during transit. He unzips it fully and sees his clothes neatly folded just as he packed them. He finds no suspicious packages tucked into the toes of his shoes.

He takes out his wash bag and looks for his razor. He has not shaved for days. His wash bag is crammed full of things he does not really need, has never made use of, but which he always takes with him. He has bath salts in there, a bath mitt, a pumice stone.

The bathroom is even smaller than he remembers. He fills the short tub, taking out the neglected bath salts and pouring them under the running water. He puts the mitt and the pumice stone on the side with his razor, undresses and gets in. It is only when he is submerged in water too hot for his sunburn that he realises he did not see the lighthouse in his suitcase.

When he gets out, his skin is very clean and soft and

sore. He drains the water, leaving behind his dead skin cells and thousands of millimetres of stubble.

Emerging from the bathroom, he expects to find his supper on the side but there is nothing there. He puts on his pyjamas and moves his suitcase from the bed to a chair and is just about to get into bed without having had his supper when he turns back to his suitcase, opens it up and looks again for his lighthouse. After searching thoroughly without finding it, he stands wondering for a few moments. He looks at his watch – it is nearly closing time. He goes to the door and looks out into the empty corridor. He does not want to get dressed again but he does not have a dressing gown. Stepping into the corridor just as he is, he goes quickly to the lift and down to the bar.

Seeing that Ester's stool is empty, he asks the girl behind the bar where Ester is. He puts the question in German and the girl's brief reply is also in German but Futh does not know enough of the language to understand what she has said. He would ask her to repeat herself but she has quickly turned back to her customer. Futh looks around and sees, sitting at a small table, the barman who refused him breakfast at the beginning of the week. He decides not to ask him about Ester, which, besides, would mean him walking across the room in his pyjamas.

He leaves the bar again, gets back into the lift and goes upstairs. After hesitating for a moment in the corridor, he walks down it to the door at the end which says 'PRIVATE'. It is a fire door. He pushes it open and goes through.

On the other side, there is a further stretch of corridor leading to another door, the entrance to a private apartment. Futh listens at the apartment door and thinks that he can hear something, a woman talking. He knocks. When there is no answer, he tries the handle. The unlocked door opens and he finds himself looking into a brightly lit hallway, at the far end of which is an open door and beyond it a room whose light is also on. He calls Ester's name. Clearly hearing someone laughing, he calls once more from the doorway and then ventures into the apartment, the door closing quietly behind him.

Futh, making his way down the hallway, calling Ester's name again, passes a small living room on one side and an even smaller kitchen on the other. There is nobody in either. He enters the end room and realises that the female voice he heard was drifting up from the street below, coming in through an open window.

Near the window, there is a bed, and Futh sits down on it to rest his aching legs while he decides what to do about his lighthouse. He supposes it could wait until morning. He could ask about it at breakfast time. But that man might be there instead of Ester, and Futh does not see him being helpful at all.

While he is thinking, he looks around, seeing the dog-eared romance on Ester's nightstand, and next to it a bottle of lotion which he picks up. Squeezing some into the palm of his hand, he tries it on his sunburn but it stings.

In the other half of the room there is an en suite bathroom which he did not notice before, but the door is open and he can see that the bathroom, whose light is off, is empty. Near the bathroom door there is a wardrobe and a dressing table, and on top of the dressing table there is a silver lighthouse. He stands up slowly and crosses the room, but as he nears the dressing table he hears someone coming into the apartment. Futh is suddenly acutely aware of being out of bounds, that while he could have explained his being on the wrong side of the private door, the fire door, there is no excuse for being discovered in Ester's bedroom in his pyjamas. Regretting his intrusion, he slips into the bathroom and pushes the door to.

The bathroom window is open and through it Futh can see the full moon. On the window sill he sees half a dozen Venus flytraps and is reminded of Gloria. He pictures her opening her kitchen door in her slippers, smiling at him and saying as she turned away, 'Come in and keep me company.'

There was, on the occasion which he is remembering, no supper. Gloria took him upstairs, into Kenny's bedroom, where she was drinking straight from a bottle of something which she said would put hairs on his chest. She went back to doing what she had been doing, going through Kenny's drawers, putting his things into a box.

'He wants all his stuff,' she said. 'All these things he never took with him, he wants them now. His dad's taking him abroad.'

'Is he?' said Futh. 'To Europe?'

'No,' she said. 'Not Europe.' She put a pile of old bike magazines in the box. 'I don't know why he wants all this junk. He can't take it with him. He wants it though. I said to him, "Just leave something here." He might want a magazine to read when he's back. He might need a jumper.' She held one up. 'This one's too small for him anyway. You have it. It will be just right for you.' She put it into Futh's hands. 'Put it on,' she said. 'Let me see you in it. It's cold outside anyway.' Futh was, in fact, feeling rather warm in Kenny's overheated bedroom. Gloria was wearing a dressing gown but it was as thin as any of her nighties. Futh put the jumper on though and Gloria looked pleased. 'There you are,' she said. He picked up a compass and Gloria said, 'Do you like that? You can have it if you want.'

She excused herself then, leaving Futh to look through Kenny's things. He put the compass in his back pocket and took an old car maintenance manual out of the box. He was planning on learning to drive as soon as he was old enough. He had fantasies about driving off into the countryside with a packet of sandwiches and a blanket, or taking his passport and driving to Dover.

After a while, Futh went looking for Gloria and found her in the bath, the bathroom door ajar. He realised that he had heard the bathwater running and had heard it stop but had not put two and two together.

'Come in,' she said. 'Come and do my back.' He stayed where he was, out on the landing, the car maintenance manual held in front of him like a shield, tight against his chest like body armour. 'Come on,' she said. 'I can't reach.' He put the manual down on the laundry basket just inside the door as he went in.

Gloria held out a loofah. 'I used to get Kenny to do this for me,' she said, putting the loofah into Futh's hand. 'I used to get him to scrub my back and give me a little shoulder rub.' She passed him the soap. 'He was always very good at it,' she said, 'very good with his hands.'

That was the last time Futh went to Gloria's house looking for Kenny.

Futh, perching on the edge of Ester's bath, looking through a narrow gap between the door and the frame, sees Ester coming into the room. He watches her, his pulse quickening. She is holding a plate of food – cold meat and boiled eggs and salad – with clingfilm over the top. She walks over to the dressing table and sets the plate down, picks up the silver lighthouse and puts it away in a drawer.

Reaching to the back of another drawer, she takes out a packet of cigarettes and a red Bic lighter, goes to the open window and lights up. Some of her smoke drifts back into the bedroom and some comes in through the bathroom window and Futh breathes it in.

He shifts slightly, knocking into the bottles lined up behind the taps, putting his hand out to stop them falling into the tub. Holding one, he unscrews the top and puts it to his nose and the smell of camphor takes him back to the dark interior of his mother's wardrobe. It is like being wrenched soul first through time.

Ester drops her cigarette butt onto the pavement below, walks back to the dressing table and puts the packet of cigarettes and the lighter away in the drawer. Picking up the plate, she leaves the room.

Again, she leaves the bedroom lights on – Futh presumes she is coming to bed after delivering the meal to his room, which will only take a minute. He stands behind Ester's bathroom door listening to her leaving, and then comes out.

He goes to the dressing table and opens one of its three drawers, looking for the silver lighthouse. The drawer is full of make-up, worn-down lipsticks, Ester's shade of pink. There is some jewellery – gold necklaces and a charm bracelet – loose in the drawer, and lots of the little boxes in which jewellery comes. One of them has lost its lid and pinned to the square of foam inside is what he initially thinks is a moth brooch, before realising that it is a moth. He touches its stilled wings before closing the drawer.

The second drawer he opens contains underwear. Near the top he finds the same pink satin knickers he found beneath his bed the week before.

In the last drawer, he finds dozens of perfume bottles – some cheap, some expensive, a few novelty bottles and cases including a blue glass skyscraper and a little wooden lighthouse, and, beside it, what is surely his silver lighthouse. He is taking it out when the slam of the apartment's front door makes him jump. Retreating once more to the dark and smoky bathroom, he feels himself trembling. He could do with relieving his bladder.

Ester, he thinks, is bound to discover him there now. Sitting down on the side of the bath, he finds that he is still holding the pink satin knickers. He has begun to worry that he is going to be asked to leave the hotel. He will have to sleep in his car and he does not have a blanket in there. And once again, he thinks, he will not get his breakfast.

In his other hand, he has the lighthouse. He is only vaguely aware that it feels unusually heavy.

He cannot see into the bedroom, there being no gap now between the door and the frame, but he hears the metallic clack of her heels on the bare floorboards as she walks into the room. The sound they make reminds him of tap dancing.

She pauses in the middle of the room before walking towards the bed, and then, after a moment, he hears her coming back to the near side of the room. She opens the wardrobe doors, and shuts them again. He hears her drumming her fingernails on the door or the side of the wardrobe as if she is standing there thinking, deciding. She moves closer to the bathroom.

Futh sits as quietly as he can in the dark, in the moonlight. For the first time since he was twelve he thinks he might wet himself. His heart is pounding, his blood rushing to the surface of his bath-softened skin. His face is burning and his pyjamas are sweaty under the arms. He looks down at his feet and breathes deeply in and out, trying to relax his toes, his arches, his ankles, inhaling and exhaling and concentrating on relaxing his calves, his knees, his thighs, his groin, feeling the warmth spreading through him.

She is standing right outside the bathroom, on the other side of the door. She is almost close enough to smell, and in the moment between the bathroom door opening and Futh looking up, the light flashing on, he smells camphor.

CHAPTER EIGHTEEN

THE FERRY

The floor, luridly carpeted to hide the vomit, tilts and sways beneath Carl's feet as he crosses the ferry lounge. When he opens the outside door, the sea air blusters in. He steps through, closing the metal door behind him.

The evening is cool; he misses his hat. The sky still has a bit of blue but the moon is out. It appears full, but in fact it was full last night and is already waning.

He looks around at the other people standing outside, scanning their faces. He is looking for the man he met on the ferry the previous weekend, who accompanied him to his mother's house in Utrecht. Carl was hoping to see him out here on the deck.

Even though they spent some hours together only a week ago, and even though Carl has thought about him since, he finds that he cannot really visualise him. He was thin, he remembers, with thinning hair. He was pale, but perhaps that was just seasickness.

He cannot even remember the man's name. It was a name which makes him think of froth, and the powdery wings of a moth. It was a name which seemed to vanish even as he heard it. He searches his memory, but the name has gone.

Carl, holding on to the railings, watches the coastline fade. The ferry, now surrounded by sea, will be in England by morning.

The conference was interesting. Contrary to what his mother insists on believing, there was no reading of crystal balls or tea leaves, only papers delivered by people with grants. He listened to speakers on the topics of telepathy, remote viewing and distant healing. What really fascinates him is the subject of premonition and precognition. It is true that he has been experimenting with tarot cards, but he does not appreciate his mother's disparaging comments. He was embarrassed by her coming to his room while they had a guest and berating him for 'messing about with those bloody cards'. Before leaving him alone she said, 'And will you be needing our coffee grounds?'

He looks around the deck once more for this man, this uneasy traveller who gave him a lift in his car. This makes him think about the car deck, its throb, its fuel stink, the metal walls and the metal floor and the strip lights on the metal ceiling, the luminous orange paint and the safety notices, the hazard warnings, the no-smoking signs and the fire extinguishers, the sirens and flashing lights. It reminds him of the underground or a submarine and turns his stomach.

Down on the car deck on the outward journey, sitting in the passenger seat of his acquaintance's car with the road atlas on his lap, waiting to go, he suddenly had this

dreadful feeling of being trapped, the sense of a disaster about to happen. It made him feel quite sick. As he turned to his companion and said, 'Do you ever get a bad feeling about something?' the ramp was lowered and there was daylight, there was the sky, and his friend was working at some tune as they sat there waiting to drive out into the brightness of the day.

ACKNOWLEDGEMENTS

Big thanks to Nick Royle for early encouragement and invaluable feedback, for astute editing and patience; to Dan for close reading and the making of many good points, for being able to sleep with the light on and being so supportive; to Wheelbarrow Grandma for Arthur's play dates; to John Oakey for the great cover; and to Jen and Chris at Salt for being such a pleasure to work with.